"This was my first book by Lisa Phillips, and it certainly didn't disappoint. The main characters felt real and carefully crafted, and their journey was both uplifting and genuine. The balance of faith was also just right, adding depth without overshadowing the story. The pacing was perfect—steady enough to keep me hooked, but never overwhelming with too much suspense."

—Lisa, GOODREADS

BURNING HEARTS

BURNING HEARTS

LISA PHILLIPS

sunrise
PUBLISHING

Burning Hearts
Chasing Fire: Alaska, Book 1

Copyright © 2025 Sunrise Media Group LLC
Print ISBN: 978-1-963372-94-6
Ebook ISBN: 978-1-963372-95-3

For more information about Lisa Phillips please access the author's web-
site at www.authorlisaphillips.com.
Published in the United States of America.
Cover Design: Sunrise Media Group LLC

To those who stand in the gap and
beat back the flames.
Thank you.

A NOTE FROM LISA

Every book is special, and some are just plain fun.
From the moment Jamie and Logan showed up
arguing in Expired Vows (Laura Conaway) I just
knew there was a story for them. They clearly had
some things to work out, and I loved digging into
their background to figure out what happened.

I hope you enjoy their story. Along with their ro-
mance and the sweetness of what has always been
between them despite the problems, it's clear that
something is happening in Alaska. But what? The
spark in book 1 ignites a flame that will carry this
plot through the series as we journey to figuring out
who these militia people are and what they're after.
No nukes – I promise! But it will be a thrill-ride
and a half for sure.

Buckle up and enjoy the ride!

ONE

LOGAN CRAWFORD ONLY SLEPT WELL in two places. On the ground on the side of a mountain, with his pack for a pillow, or in a short takeoff and landing fixed-wing aircraft.

Smoke in the air.

Logan leaned back against his seat, the vibration so familiar now that he hardly rested when he couldn't hear the rumble of an airplane engine or feel the hard ground of the backcountry.

This was what he'd been born to do.

He'd discovered in the last few years that he could fight fire anywhere, but he needed the rush of jumping. The flap of the parachute above him. There was nothing like the feel of falling through the air. Couldn't find that in a town like Last Chance County, fighting residential fires as part of a rescue squad with his twin, Bryce. Being back home had been great, but there was nothing like smokejumping.

"I see the header!" their spotter, Mark, called out down the plane. Then he trained his binoculars on the copilot window, his attention on their target while his long gray hair hung down his back.

Logan glanced at the cockpit, also occupied by the pilot, who was a retiree who'd flown for JPATS for years. According to Neil, flying a bunch of rowdy smokejumpers wasn't so different from flying transports between judicial districts and correctional institutions for the US Marshals. Thankfully, Neil didn't have to fear for his life if something went wrong.

At least, not beyond the normal perils of being a wildland pilot.

The smokejumper boss, Jade Ransom, hefted herself out of her seat and went to speak with Neil and Mark. She'd been Logan's jump boss at the end of last season in Montana and had moved back up here with her boyfriend Crispin in the offseason.

They weren't the only ones who'd come north.

"Almost there, right?"

Logan glanced at the smokejumper in the seat next to him. Orion Price was another one of the people he knew from Ember, Montana. A rookie smokejumper this year, and with his brown hair and blue eyes, the kid looked like a college student. Young, but not as young as one of their hotshots, Mack. "Nervous?"

Orion said, "You ever look out the window of the plane and wonder why you thought this was a good idea?"

No way. Nervous, but trying to hide it. "You trained plenty for this and passed the qualifiers," Logan said over the drone of the plane engine. "You wouldn't be here if you hadn't earned it by proving you can do the job."

Orion nodded sharply.

Across the plane, on the other side of the aisle, Cadee and Tori chatted to each other—which involved a lot of close talking, trying to whisper but also hear each other over the airplane engine, and the occasional glance at Vince.

JoJo sat with her head back against his seat in the row in front of Cadee and Tori. Another Montana transplant up here to see what Alaska had to offer.

Skye sat in the row in front of Logan, with Vince next to her. Skye was Alaska born and raised, same as Cadee. Vince had been on the smokejumper team in Montana last summer.

Jade turned from the cockpit and her conversation with the pilot and spotter. "Okay, rookies. Give me streamers."

Jade led the group down the aisle to the back of the plane and rotated the lever to open the door.

Wind rushed in, bringing a stronger scent of smoke with it.

Tori and Orion tossed streamers out the door—weighted crepe paper that told them which way the wind blew and how fast they would descend before they hit the ground. Vince wasn't a rookie, but he sent his own flying out. It was in all their natures to be a bit of a control freak.

Enough. Logan levered out of his seat with his gear and went to the other side of the plane to get a look out the window. If he was gonna fight this fire, he needed to see where it was first.

Skye did the same at the window of the row in front. "I told you that storm last night was gonna kick it off. Lightning strikes." She let out a whistle and shook her head. "Fifteen acres at least." She pointed. "See the ridge line? It's starting to wake up."

Logan smirked. "Yeah, I wonder why I didn't take your bet and risk doing kitchen cleanup in the mess hall for two weeks."

She shoved his shoulder over the seat back, the same way his sister did to him and his twin brother Bryce.

Logan spotted the header. The plume of smoke that snaked up into the wide Alaskan sky was their destination. The jump spot would land them two miles southeast of it. Northwest of the base, in the shadow of Denali Mountain.

He said, "We need to put this fire out before it spreads all the way to town." Not to mention the homesteads in its path.

Over the last few years, he had fought wildfires in a lot of places across Australia, Montana, and even parts of Canada. There was nowhere like Alaska. The whole landscape was like the proverbial black widow woman—beautiful and alluring, but underneath the surface, it was trying to kill you.

And not just the fires.

This one might be fifteen acres now, but by tonight it would spread to a whole lot more. So they'd parachute down and cut a line. Starve it of fuel. Make the world a little bit safer. One battle at a time. One jump at a time.

One breath at a time.

His firefighting mentor's voice echoed in his ears.

Skye said, "What did the sheriff tell you?"

Logan turned from the window and sat, weighed down by more than his gear. "Hasn't seen Tristan, hasn't spoken to Jamie. If she really is looking for her brother, Jamie could be who-knows-where right now."

"But someone saw her at the Midnight Sun Saloon a week ago."

He shrugged. "Maybe they were mistaken."

Or he'd missed her.

Skye patted his shoulder. "Want me to talk to Rio?"

Her husband, the FBI agent? "Pretty sure he has better things to do than look for a woman who doesn't want me to find her."

Jade made her way down the aisle of the plane, cutting off whatever Skye was about to say. "Turning final, sixteen hundred feet!"

Every smokejumper on the plane yelled back, "Copy that."

Logan glanced at Skye, who grinned at him. He wanted to roll his eyes, but she knew he loved this as much as she did. Lived for it.

They lined up at the door.

Vince and Tori. Cadee and Orion. Logan and Skye lined up behind them. Then JoJo and Jade. Partners. Teammates.

Who knew what this summer season would bring? If he found Jamie, great. He'd do what he'd come to Alaska to do and tell her how he felt—how he'd always felt. If not, he still planned to jump headlong into every fire that came at them with the reassurance this was what God had put him on this earth to do.

Their spotter, Mark, came to the door, where hot wind rushed in to beat at their jumpsuits. He pushed out two crates. Supply drops. Tools.

Gear. Medical supplies just in case. Not much, but enough it might be the difference between life and death if something happened out here in this forbidding landscape.

Logan adjusted his straps and checked the rest of his gear. "'The Lord himself goes before you and will be with you.'"

Skye said, "'He will never leave you nor forsake you.'"

Vince grunted, but the rest of them knew the drill by now. This was who Logan was these days.

Orion was the one who said, "'Do not be afraid.'"

Logan finished the words from Deuteronomy by saying, "'Do not be discouraged.'" Voicing it sent an unwelcome note ringing in his heart. He hadn't found Jamie yet. *I don't want to be discouraged.*

But the fact was, he'd come to Alaska for a very particular reason—and it wasn't to get up close and personal with the local wildlife. Or to face any of the fights they had in Montana, running from bad guys who wanted a war between the US and Russia. Searching for the truth hidden in the Kootenai National Forest.

This was about a girl, of course.

The one that got away—because he'd left her. Broken it off. Walked away.

One in a line of mistakes where Jamie was concerned. He was here to get her back. Or to keep her safe, if she really was traipsing all over Copper Mountain trying to find her brother.

Logan pushed all those frustrating thoughts away. If he didn't focus up, he was going to hit the ground and become a permanent part of Alaska.

Jade said, "Ready?"

Logan nodded.

The spotter yelled, "Your static line is clear."

He held on. Felt the tap.

Jumped.

Logan peered through the grate of his helmet while wind whipped the high collar on the back of his jumpsuit.

Above him, the rectangular chute that had been pulled open by the static line fluttered. The thing that saved him every time he jumped—by the grace of God.

How sweet the sound ... of a parachute in the wind.

He looked from his chute to the plume of smoke where the fire ate up vegetation, then to the snowcapped peak of Denali and adjusted to land on course. Green hills rose up beneath him. The river, with its ice-cold snow-runoff water. Crags and cliffs where the earth tumbled down into the drink. Clusters of Alaska spruce trees broken up by red roofs and blue-capped barns.

Dirt roads that would be their exit—once they hiked far enough that they found one.

The wind current changed.

He fought with the toggles, but a particularly hot gust whipped him over and sent him west toward the densely packed trees of the forest on that side. The area the fire was *not* supposed to reach.

Logan gritted his teeth and struggled against the fierceness of nature. The last thing he wanted was to get hung up on a tree.

Everyone else headed for the jump spot, apparently not needing to battle this gust that'd caught him. He wasn't a rookie! He expelled a shout of frustration.

Apparently nothing was going to go right for him up in Alaska.

Jamie Winters gripped the satellite phone against her cheek, backpack on, trudging through the Alaska backwoods like this was any other hike with her best friend Kelsey in Last Chance County. Not a last-ditch effort to save her brother's sorry hide.

She said, "I took a look at the early projections last night. I sent over some thoughts. Overall, I think the concept for the tracker ring is a good one, and it seems like a solid investment for us."

The board of directors on the other end of

the line, with her on speaker on the phone in the middle of their conference room table where she usually sat with them, was *her* board of directors. Friends. Colleagues. Mentors. People she kept around to be a sanity check in her company.

Samuel, her chief operations officer, said, "Solid is what we were thinking too."

Jamie stopped to catch her breath. While the sun lit the sky, it wasn't all that warm. She'd opted for a long-sleeved sweat-wicking shirt, cargo pants, and hiking boots that were now giving her blisters. *Wearing new shoes was a bad idea.* She was so far out of her element it was throwing her off.

This definitely wasn't a city-outskirts hike up some leisurely hill in the foothills around Last Chance County.

No, this was Alaska.

She was climbing a *mountain*, of all things.

Samuel continued, "It's new, but testing has been promising. If they're gonna get it off the ground, they need solid backing. Which is where you come in."

We was more like it. Even if she was the one who'd started the company, it was theirs now. She hadn't worked alone in finance and investments for nearly a decade. Still, she was too out of breath from hiking to say more than, "I agree."

They weren't going to accept altruism as a reason to funnel millions of their capital into brand-new tech. But Jamie liked that it allowed firefighters, both ones who worked within city limits and those who fought wildfires, to be located if anything ever happened to them.

The fact she'd been in longing—she refused to call it love—with a firefighter for years was beside the point.

The tracker ring technology had far broader applications than only aiding those who fought against the destruction of flames for a living.

This wasn't about Logan.

She'd read enough memoirs of smokejumpers, hotshots, and firefighters to have decided to "cut a line" around those feelings—or so they called it. She'd starved that part of her heart of fuel so the fire that had at one point burned hot and heavy for Logan Crawford had since exhausted itself and gone out.

These days it was barely a smolder.

"That's great news, Ms. Winters," Samuel said. "I'll send the memo that we have decided to fund the project, and inform the woman who created it that we're giving it the green light." He paused. "Unless that's the reason you've been up in Alaska these past weeks? You're close to where I believe her base is. At least, according to the GPS on the tracker ring you have on your person."

Jamie reached the top of the ridge and stopped at the apex of the deer trail she'd been walking up, refusing to get distracted by the amazing view. Or the hint of smoke on the breeze and the cloud cover that might be more the haze of wildfire smoke than an indication that precipitation was in the forecast.

Of course they knew where she was.

"Not that I meant to locate you. I just happened to log in to the system to take a look and saw you'd signed one out."

"It's fine, Samuel. Probably a good thing, actually."

She didn't keep much of her personal life from her board. She just didn't work that way. No one else in her life whom she would consider a friend or acquaintance knew what she did—not really. It was either boring to them or too complex to fully understand when no one wanted to know that much about niche investing anyway.

But the people she worked with? Jamie trusted Samuel implicitly.

The rest of the board could find her whenever, wherever, if they needed something. She was always available, because she'd learned the hard way what happened when she took her hands off the reins. Too often they found out much too late that they'd hired someone who couldn't be trusted.

Samuel said, "I believe the wildland smoke-jumper who created the tech, Jade Ransom, is a team leader with the Midnight Sun smokejumpers. Their base isn't too far from your current location—at least, according to Alaska standards."

Jamie wasn't going to pay them a visit, even for the purpose of shaking the hand of her newest client. She much preferred to be the anonymous CEO behind the curtain. "Anything else on the schedule?"

Her CFO cleared his throat and went over the effect of a server going down the month before. A problem their tech people had solved quickly, but the ramifications were still being unpacked. At times ad nauseum.

Jamie half listened to him talking and took in the vista in front of her. Sprawling hills on the other side of the valley stretched up as if they were trying to compete with Denali for superiority but came up far short.

On the valley floor, there seemed to be some kind of fenced compound. Multiple buildings, huge metal structures, Quonset huts. Mobile homes and cabins, vehicles everywhere—ATVs, UTVs that looked like hyped-up off-road golf carts, and trucks. So many trucks. She spotted a couple of loose dogs roaming around. Almost every person down there seemed to be male, though she did see a couple of women.

"Uh . . . that's everything, Ms. Winters."

She focused back on her call. "Thank you, Mr. Penning."

Samuel adjourned the meeting and told her not to hang up. She held the phone to her ear, the bulky satellite unit warm against her cheek. Jamie watched the movement below, trying to figure out their organizational pattern. Like watching ants in a terrarium.

How was she going to find her brother in there, short of marching in the front gate and demanding to see him?

"Can you hear me?" Samuel's voice was a lot closer now, like he'd taken her off speaker and held the handset to his ear.

Jamie looked at the dusty toes of her hiking boots. "Yes. And before you ask, I'm fine."

"At least you didn't try to tell me that you know what you're doing."

They both knew she was in over her head. "Thank you for keeping things going while I'm out of town."

She worked from home a lot, in the converted basement of her upper-middle-class house. Because no one needed to come over to a mansion to watch a movie and eat pizza. Jamie had always wanted to be normal. To be treated like everyone else. If that meant she had to hide some parts of who she was . . .

What was the problem? It was her business, not theirs.

Samuel said, "Are you really sure your brother warrants this much effort?"

"You already know the answer to that."

"I wish you'd taken my advice about a security team."

Because she wanted to be a lone woman in Alaska surrounded by a team of expensive bodyguards? Talk about obvious. There was no way to slip in and out without many people noticing, or keep a low profile in general, if she had a team of people on her twenty-four seven.

Samuel sighed because she wasn't going to argue. She also wasn't going to tell him she would be all right no matter what. Jamie just didn't want to drag anyone else into her family mess.

Her relationship with Logan had proven to her that people outside her family didn't understand their dynamic. He hadn't liked the fact she was all in to help her mother and her brother. She cared about them too much to let them throw their lives away, and if that meant getting messy trying to pull either her addict mother or her wayward brother out of whatever jam they were in, she would do it.

"Please, be careful. We don't want to lose you," Samuel said. "After all, if you disappear, it will affect the bottom line."

Jamie grinned. He cared. He just knew getting soft wasn't what their company needed. "Of course. I wouldn't want to affect next quarter's projections."

Then again, if she did die, all her money would go to kids' programs and the women's shelter in Last Chance County. So it wasn't as if she would be a loss to the world. More like a net gain.

"See you soon."

"Bye, Samuel." Jamie ended the call and stowed the phone in her backpack. She was settling it back on her shoulders when a twig snapped behind her. Jamie spun to the sound.

Three men emerged from the trees. Two hung back and one strode in front, his expression dark and menacing. They all wore what seemed to be the uniform in Alaska. Jeans and boots, heavy shirt—probably insulated. The scent of sweat and hot, clammy skin hung around them along with the distinct smell of tobacco.

The man in front towered over her, dark hair smashed to his forehead and damp with sweat. "Lookie what we have here, boys."

One of the men who'd hung back snickered.

Jamie wasn't without ways to protect herself but had to wonder if acting helpless would get her into the compound where she could find her brother. She didn't want to know what might happen to her inside that fence. "I'm not here to tangle with you guys."

"Shame," the leader said. "I like to tangle with a woman. Especially one as good-looking as you."

He scanned her face, probably as sweaty as his. She always got red cheeks when she exerted herself—a product of her fair skin. Her dark hair was braided so that the twin braids hung behind her ears and down over her shoulders. She'd always thought her eyes were too big for her face.

He reached out and tugged on one braid. "What are you doin' out here, girl?"

She should slap his hand away, but everything in her said that would only escalate things. She should pray but couldn't find the words. Now wasn't the time to wonder how long it had been since she'd asked God for help. Not just the rote prayers that came with Sunday services but actual conversation with God.

A note of grief washed over her.

Jamie lifted her chin. "I'm looking for my brother."

"You don't need him." The guy shifted closer, his hand still around the hair tie on her braid. Far too near. "I can show you a good time. You'll forget all about him."

Jamie swallowed.

One of the guys behind him said, "Uh, Snatch? We're supposed to be back already."

Snatch—which had to be a nickname, and Jamie didn't want to know what it meant—spun around to his buddy. "Shut up, Crew. I'm workin' on somethin'."

"Just bring her with us." Crew strode past them, his expression impassive as if he didn't care either way. "I'm not gonna be any later than we already are."

The third guy followed him.

Neither one of them was her brother.

Snatch tugged on her braid. "Let's go, girlie. I gotta check in with the boss, and then you and me can see what happens next."

Jamie shivered. "I don't think that's—"

He grabbed her wrist, squeezing hard enough the bones hurt. "Get walkin'."

TWO

LOGAN GRITTED HIS TEETH, STEERING with the toggles. He picked a spot on the ground before the tree line where something had flashed in the sunlight. He aimed for it like a beacon, aptly named because the red metal glinted in the sun. Not a house or cabin...

It was a car.

Same color as hers. As if God would land him right in her path.

Jamie.

I know You don't work like that. I'm not just going to bump into her. Alaska is a big place, even if she's nearby.

But the need to see her—to know she was safe—gave him what he needed to focus. To fight the wind with enough strength he landed just shy of the trees. His boots hit the dirt road hard, and he caught the tumble, only a little wince. Pretty glad no one saw that. *It was the wind's fault.*

Logan shoved off his helmet and got his chute gathered up, both of which he tucked in his pack-out bag.

He tugged the radio from the same bag and turned the dial. He couldn't see anyone else on the team now. Had they all made it to the jump spot on the other side of that hill? "Jade, this is Logan. Come in."

He stomped off the frustration by heading over to look at the car. Not even the same make and model as Jamie's. Abandoned, like the cabin behind him. A wreck, with the roof caved in and half the porch under debris. No one had lived here in years.

The radio crackled in his hand. "Yeah, Logan. Can you hold, over?"

Logan frowned. "What's going on, Jade?"

He leaned on the car and peered in the window. Not an abandoned vehicle. Someone who'd run out of gas, maybe? *A terrifying thought in the middle of nowhere.* He peered in the window and spotted a duffel on the backseat. The paperwork on the dash indicated it was a rental, but he knew that bag.

Oh no.

"Vince got hung up on a tree, but Hammer is cutting him down. You good?"

No, he was not good. *This is Jamie's car.* He looked around, turning in a circle. No one in sight. Just the deadly backcountry of Alaska.

"Logan, you good?"

Her question jogged him out of his . . . blind terror? Pretty accurate. "I'm good." Jamie was not. "There's something I need to do. I'm gonna be late catching up."

He'd never broken protocol like this before. *Lord, don't let me regret this.* He could only trust that God had led him here.

"Logan, what are you doing?" Skye.

He winced. "I'll catch up. I promise."

"You better. Over."

Question was, after he'd been looking for her for weeks, how long was it going to take to actually find Jamie out here?

And would she be alive when he did?

Logan pulled off his jumpsuit, shoving the heavy material into his pack. He left the bigger bag by the car so he could look around the nearby area unencumbered by everything he'd brought. Though he did put a few things in his pants pockets. Slid the radio on his belt. Map and compass?

Nah.

He knew the area just fine. There was nothing out here.

Logan circled the car. Tried the doors. She'd locked it, which meant Jamie had intentionally parked here. At least, barring another circumstance he didn't want to contemplate right now.

Should he report the abandoned vehicle to the local sheriff?

In the trees, about ten feet from the car, he spotted a path that snaked up the hill. Definitely not man-made. If Jamie was out here and she'd encountered a dangerous animal, Logan absolutely wanted to know. Even if it would only be so he had closure.

Lord, You brought me this far.

He figured it wouldn't take long to climb the hill as the animals did when they wandered across the land. The team had raced up steeper hills than this, training hard for the grueling work they did. His muscles needed to move after being cooped up in the plane with all that gear on.

Logan took off running.

Halfway, he realized the path was longer than he'd thought, but he found the top of the ridge after nearly fifteen minutes of a solid nine-minute-mile pace, which was his usual easy run. When he bent over, hands on his knees, his legs shook. Laps of the runway in sneakers were one thing. Running uphill in boots was another.

He straightened, hands behind his head and

his elbows splayed. From up here, he'd be able to send intel that could help the others fight the fire.

But instead of an open valley below him, he spotted some kind of compound. The fenced buildings bustled with people moving between structures. Two trucks drove in from the east, admitted through the gate, which was rolled closed behind them.

The fire was to the west, where he could barely see the smoke, but headed this way. The occupants of this valley probably couldn't even see how near it was. They likely had no idea how close to danger they were, as the air currents seemed to be sending the smoke over the top of the valley rather than down into it, acting like an inversion, where the cloud cover sat like a lid on a bowl and below was only stagnant air.

Logan keyed his radio. "This is Logan, does anyone copy?"

The response came a few seconds later. "I copy you, Logan." That was JoJo. "We're on the trail, headed for the fire. How long are you gonna be? I can give you our coordinates."

He wouldn't be catching up. Not with what he was looking at right now. "I found a compound in a valley to the north. Looks like a lot of people down there, and the fire is headed east, right toward them."

After a long pause, Jade got on. "It's not on the map."

Logan didn't remember talk about a compound in their briefing. "Should I head down and advise them to evacuate?"

Never mind if Jamie was down there or not. Logan wouldn't be able to walk away without telling these people—whoever they were—that their lives were in danger if the fire spread to the valley in front of him.

"I'll let the sheriff know there are people at your location. He might be interested to know since none of us were aware."

"Copy that." Logan would have to walk all the way down this hill to even get near enough to speak to someone. The closest people seemed to be a couple of guys with a woman between them. As he watched, one of the men shoved the woman to the other, who grasped her.

Logan winced. Not the kind of people he wanted to try and reason with, but everyone deserved to be warned if their lives were in danger. He could advise them to leave, but if they didn't want to go, he couldn't force it. He would need local law enforcement to roust them all out—or to at least do so with a little more authority than Logan had.

The man dragged the woman to a building and in a side door.

"Go ahead and advise them to evacuate, which they already should have done." Jade didn't sound happy. "But I want you with us by lunchtime, Logan. Got it?"

"Got it, boss." Logan lowered the radio and set off down the hill. He was going to get written up for not heading for them right away after he landed, but the fact Jade hadn't sent a rescue party to help him meant she trusted him, at least a little. "I'll be there."

"If you need backup, call it in. But we have a fire to fight."

"Copy that. Out."

He jogged a little, but mostly fast walked. Not just for the woman he'd seen being menaced by these guys. All of the people down here deserved a chance to live—to face the truth of the Bible and find redemption. Every person on earth got a shot at a second chance. He'd learned that the hard way after running from God for years. He'd finally surrendered his life on the same night his twin brother, Bryce, had. At a church service, where the pastor had talked about a shepherd who'd left ninety-nine sheep to find one lost lamb.

In a way, that was probably what Jamie thought she was doing for her brother. Wherever she'd ended up.

Down there?

What a horrifying thought.

Logan made it to the gate. "Hey, bro! Gotta talk to you."

The guy took his cigarette out of his mouth, a rifle strapped to hang across his back. He slid the gate open enough for Logan to slip through. "Whatcha want, hotshot?"

He was a smokejumper, but this wasn't the time to correct the guy. The uniforms were the same, with a Midnight Sun Wildland Firefighter patch on the left arm. "Fire is west of here, and it's headed this way. Y'all need to evacuate while there's still time."

The guy took another drag on his cigarette, about to speak when another man joined them. The guy immediately launched into conversation about something funny, given the laughter in his tone. "Snatch claimed her. She told him her name is Jamie, which is a dumb name for a girl, but whatever."

Logan glanced at the guy. "What did you just say?"

Jamie's back hit the wall. Snatch had dragged her in here despite her protests and attempts to explain. And her trying to bargain with him. "I really need to find my brother."

She didn't have many options for getting herself out of this. They'd taken all her things. Except they had no idea the tracker on her right index finger wasn't just an ordinary ring.

Too bad no one knew she was in trouble, but at least her colleagues knew where she was.

This was going to come down to the self-defense moves she'd learned in the class she'd taken after Samuel had found out she didn't know how to fight off an attacker.

Snatch pressed against her. "We can talk after." His breath wafted across her face.

"I need to talk to him." Was he even going to listen to her? "You see, my brother just inherited money from our grandfather."

Snatch hit the brakes on his attempt to woo her into whatever he had planned up against this wall in a random office. Because she'd mentioned money?

The room had a single metal desk. No shelves or books or artwork on the walls. A single bulb hung from the middle of the ceiling. For some reason, there was a fire extinguisher on the wall behind the door—minus the tag that meant it had been inspected. Logan was the one who'd taught her that they needed to be checked regularly.

Now back it on up there, buddy. She tried to smile. "I have to tell him how much he's gonna get paid. That's why I came here. To tell him about the money."

"How about you don't," Snatch said, "and you and I split it?"

"Well, that wouldn't be fair now, would it?" She tried to smile.

He grinned, teeth slightly yellowed from life in the wilds away from the plastic, bleached culture of suburbs, lattes, and shiny SUVs. Jamie didn't fit in either and had given up trying to figure out why a long time ago. "Who said things have to be fair?"

The door opened. One of those guys from the hill poked his head in. *Crew.* He sure wasn't going to rescue her. "Snatch, boss wants to talk to you. Says whatever you have going on can wait."

Snatch whirled around. "Watch her. Make sure she goes nowhere."

Crew nodded.

"Not like you have it in you to do anything." Snatch strode out, laughing to himself. "Choir boy."

Crew's jaw flexed. He stared at nothing for a couple of seconds, then said, "T!"

Her brother came into the room, and Crew stepped out, closing the door behind him. As if they'd planned this entire interruption and got rid of Snatch with a distraction so he'd leave the room.

"Tristan!" She tried to keep her voice low but rushed to him with her arms open.

He held up his hand. "What are you doing here?"

Jamie stopped. "I came here to find out what *you're* doing here, of course. To tell you that Mom is doing . . . better. To help you if you needed it."

Why didn't he look happy to see her?

"You shouldn't have come." He sniffed. A hunk of brown hair fell over his shoulder, and she had to resist the urge to smooth it back. She'd done that when he was little—fixed his hair for church. Made sure he'd brushed his teeth and that he always ate his breakfast before school and that he'd done his homework. All the while, her mom had been passed out on the bathroom floor—or not even home yet.

When their mom had been there, Jamie had still done all those things.

You shouldn't have come.

"What are you talking about, Tristan? Of course I came."

She always did, and no matter what Logan had said, it wasn't codependency. Who else would reach out a hand to them when they were knocked down? She and Tristan had only ever had each other.

Sure, God had probably saved them from some huge disasters, but it was hard to be thankful when she had no idea what *might've* happened. What disaster He might have averted.

41

"You don't understand who these people are, J." Tristan shook his head, a scruff of beard on his jaw. He was dressed in the same Alaska backcountry uniform as the rest of them. Jeans, a shirt, and boots. "It's not that you shouldn't have come to Alaska or come looking for me. I figured you would eventually. But they took my phone so I couldn't call out. I couldn't warn you what would happen when you did."

She'd been worried before, but this was a whole new level. "Who are these people?"

"You don't wanna know." He squeezed the bridge of his nose. "I can't leave right now."

"Of course you can! They can't keep you here against your will. We can both go." Although, they'd shut her in this room, and it didn't seem like *she* could leave anytime soon. If she pushed it, would they release her?

She'd done what she'd come here to do. Who cared about all the stuff in her pack? She could replace it all. But her brother? She couldn't replace him.

"Come with me." She touched Tristan's elbow, everything in her screaming for him to believe they needed to go. Now.

"I'm not done here. I can't leave." Tristan sighed. "I'm sorry I couldn't contact you in time to tell you not to come here."

He'd known she would. That's what it was like

with family—they understood what you needed. In her case, it was seeing that the people she loved were okay.

But then he stepped back. "I'll ask Crew to help get you out. He's one of them, but he's not the same. I can't explain it, he's just different. He'll help us."

"You think I'm gonna leave you here?"

Tristan's expression hardened. "You can't stay, and I can't leave until I work out how to stop whatever they're doing. I haven't even figured all of it out yet! So I guess that means we're at an impasse."

"I didn't come all this way to turn around and leave again." She wasn't going to go without him. If these people were into something, then no doubt it was dangerous.

He ran a hand through his hair. "I could give you a number. Call it twice and hang up. I'll know you got back to town okay. Then I want you to go back to the Lower 48. Go back to Last Chance County and don't come back here. I'll call you when I can."

"You can't possibly—"

"The longer I stand here talking to you, the more likely we're gonna get caught."

And yet, with all this talking, what had he actually told her? Not much. Barely anything.

Before she could argue, he stepped away. Jamie

didn't want to lose him again. She tugged the ring off her finger and hurried up behind him. "I can't believe you're staying." She didn't want to say this, but she had to get close enough. He really wasn't going to leave this place. "You know you can't trust these people, right?"

Jamie slipped the ring in his jacket pocket. Not perfect, but it would have to do. This was Alaska, right? He would keep his coat on.

Lord . . .

The prayer tasted stale in her mouth. She didn't even know what to say and was only asking for help because she had nothing else right now.

"Wait for Crew. He'll get you out."

Jamie pressed her lips together.

Tristan gave her one last look and shut the door. Jamie whirled around. She shook out her hands, her heart pounding in her chest. He was seriously going to stay here? Because he had to *do something*? Her brother made no sense—and it wasn't the first time. He probably couldn't leave because he owed someone money and he had to do a favor in exchange for payment.

Jamie fisted her hands by her sides. As if she was going to wait for a man she didn't trust to come and save her. If she wanted something done, the only person she'd ever had to rely on was herself. And that was exactly how she was going to get out of here.

She flung the door open.

Crew stood in the doorway, the same look on his face as Snatch when he came at her. "Going somewhere?"

Shivers rolled down her spine. She lifted her chin. "I thought you were supposed to help me get out."

His expression broke, just a fraction.

Then something swung out behind him and smacked him in the back of the head. Jamie covered her mouth with her hands, trying to muffle the scream.

Crew slumped to the floor, and another man stepped into view.

Logan.

What on earth . . .

The last man she'd expected to see when she was looking for her brother. Alaska was supposed to be a way for someone to escape the life they'd left behind. And here he was, with a determined expression on his face. One that looked an awful lot like the expression he'd worn that night at Backdraft.

It's over, Jamie. I'm sorry. I can't carry your whole family, and you shouldn't either.

Logan stared at her. "Jamie!"

She shook her head. "What are you doing here?" This made no sense. He was working in Montana, not up here.

"Looking for you." He held out his hand. "Come on. We've got to run!"

Like he was here to save her? Butting in. Deciding how things should be—as usual. She shook her head. "I'm trying to rescue Tristan."

Logan looked around the room. "He isn't here. It's time your brother saved himself."

THREE

SHE DIDN'T TAKE HIS HAND. AND after he had hit that guy over the head? Total hero stuff—and she just stood there staring at him like he was the last person she'd expected to see in Alaska.

Logan figured they didn't have more than a couple of seconds to get out of here. The minute the guys out front had mentioned Jamie, he'd covered his reaction with some inane conversation. Talked to them about evacuating and even made it all the way to a meeting in the boss's office. Brian Howards dressed like all the rest, he was just thirty years older.

Decades of experience surviving apparently didn't mean he would listen to reason.

Logan doubted these guys would even evacuate if the state police and local federal law enforcement showed up with riot gear and ordered them out. If that happened, it would likely only end with a standoff, Waco style.

All because these guys didn't want to leave their stuff.

You think we don't know about wildfires? We've done what we need to. Even if the fire gets close, we'll be fine.

Or so the guy thought.

Logan had tried to explain about the dangers of smoke inhalation, but apparently, all the possessions they intended to protect were more valuable than people to this guy. Brian Howards probably figured he'd just go to town and recruit some more guys for his militia if he lost anyone.

That had to be what this place was. A shared compound of guys who all wanted the same thing—to live under their own rules and not the law of the land. Armed and looking for freedom in all the wrong places.

Jamie lowered her hands from her mouth. She'd been stunned into inactivity for a second, but now she said, "You seriously think I'm going to leave Tristan?"

He looked down at the man on the floor, then said to her, "Come on."

He grasped her hand and tugged her from the room, down the hall. She was really here. *Thank You.* Because it seemed like God had brought him here right when she needed him. The perfect timing that could only be His.

Now they just had to get out of here.

Logan heard voices behind them.

Jamie whispered, "Someone is coming."

And they would find an unconscious man in the hallway.

He grabbed the nearest handle, prayed there was no one on the other side of the door, and rushed in. An empty room with long metal tables against one wall. Stacked chairs. Maps all along another wall. A briefing room?

He turned to close the door, catching it before it clicked shut. In the gap between the door and the frame, he watched two men walk into the hall, saw the moment they realized their colleague was down. One crouched by him, saying something to the other, younger man before he nodded and left.

The guy by the door looked into the room where Jamie had been. Logan prayed they figured she had hit that guy herself and made a run for it. He eased the door shut as quietly as he could and went to her. Jamie stood in front of the wall of maps, looking at the markings. On the right side, down the margin, someone had written a long string of numbers.

"We should be okay here for now. But it won't be long before they search every inch of this place for us." He touched her shoulder.

The sweat-wicking shirt she wore stretched across her back. Cargo pants and hiking boots completed the outfit. She looked rumpled and tired, strands of hair now coming out of her braids, and it made him want to tug her to him for a hug.

Affection had never been the problem between them. The problem had always been other people. The fact that she'd drop everything to help her family, spend thousands of dollars she probably didn't have on rehab for her mom and—case in point—put herself in danger to help Tristan.

"You're sorry?" She stared at him, tears gathering in her eyes. "I feel sorry for you. I guess your family is so perfect that no one needs anyone. Must be hard, living up to the Crawford standard."

"As soon as the coast is clear, we need to run."

She turned to him, a frown creasing her brows. "I want to get out of here *now*. Just say when." She sighed. "I can't believe Tristan wants to stay."

"He's here? I figured you were looking for him and these guys grabbed you." He'd thought he was her hero, rescuing her from men who had abducted her. Dangerous men who probably cooked meth in one of those outbuildings. Who had a cache of weapons and a plan to destabi-lize . . . something on that map she'd been looking at.

He didn't plan to stick around long enough to find out all of it.

"He said he can't leave yet."

Logan put his hand on her shoulder. "But you can."

And she *should*. Who knew what that guy would've done to her if Logan hadn't intervened? She didn't need to waste any more time trying to rescue her brother when Tristan seemed bent on ruining his own life.

"The second you saw this place, you should've turned right around and left."

She brushed his hand off her shoulder. "They'd already spotted me. You think I came in the front gate by choice? How did you get in here? Are you following me?" She shook her head. "Why are you even *in* Alaska?"

"I'm a smokejumper up here." As if he was going to tell her that he'd only come up to the Midnight Sun crew because he'd heard she was up here looking for her brother. "There's a fire to the west, and it's headed this way." Logan glanced at his watch, then touched the radio clipped to his belt. "I came here to warn these guys they need to evacuate. Then I need to catch up with my team."

Her gaze moved from his radio and swept up his uniform. A slight pink blush touched her cheeks.

Yeah, attraction had never been their problem. *Like what you see?*

"Look," Logan said, "if Tristan doesn't want to go, then you can't exactly make him. It's time to go back to town and get yourself safe. Otherwise he'll drag you into something you can't get out of."

Her gaze hardened. "So that's your deal, Mr. Smokejumper Hero? You get to swoop in and rescue me, tell me how to live my life, and then walk off into the sunset? Hmm. Seems like we've had this discussion before."

And he knew exactly where it'd happened.

In the Backdraft Bar and Grill in Last Chance County. Seemed like forever ago, and at the same time, not that long.

"I guess we're done, then." He took a step back. "For good this time."

"Yeah, I guess we are."

After that, he'd tried to forget all about her.

Hadn't worked.

"You're right." He folded his arms across his chest. "But that doesn't mean I'm going to leave you here to face whatever these guys want to do to you alone. And it won't change the fact I came up here to find you . . . so that we could see if there's still a chance. For us."

She stared at him.

"I need to know."

"You came all this way to find out?"

Logan's chest tightened. Did he want to be the guy who had to admit he couldn't let go?

"Look, I appreciate that you care enough to make sure I'm safe, but—"

He could hear the "thanks but no thanks" coming a mile off. Since he didn't want to *actually* hear it, he cut her off. "So, where is Tristan? Is he helping you get out?"

"As a matter of fact—"

Over by the door, a man cleared his throat.

Logan spun around, berating himself for being unaware someone had come into the room. Tristan stood there, a blank look on his face. Probably because he knew exactly what Logan thought of him. Before the holidays last year, a buddy had told Logan that Tristan had been involved in an incident with Benson PD at their community college. Now he was wanted for questioning by more than one agency.

Tristan looked at Jamie and held out a backpack and a busted satellite phone. "I found these. Figured you'd want to take them with you."

She rushed over. "Oh, they totally smashed it. I guess that's no surprise."

"They went through your stuff as well, but unless you had cash in your wallet, they didn't take anything."

Logan glanced at Tristan. "You mean they have her name and they know who she is now?"

Tristan shrugged. "So we get her out of here and somewhere safe."

At least they were in agreement about that.

Logan moved to see the damage to her satellite phone, but she turned and used the edge of a metal table to break the unit even more. She drew something out with two fingers—a SIM card. She slipped it into her pocket but left the phone on the table.

"Let's go." She took the pack and touched her brother's arm. "Please come with us."

Tristan's expression then was a lot like hers. Impassive. Unshakeable. "I can't. And I don't have enough information to explain it, but I'll be okay. Don't worry about me."

Logan wanted to roll his eyes. "She came all the way to Alaska to save your hide."

They both looked at him.

Logan lifted his hands and backed off. He went to the door and peeked out through the crack but didn't see anyone. Maybe his trip up here had been pointless, same as Jamie's.

While the siblings whispered to each other behind him, he couldn't help wondering if this was God's way of finally getting him to let her go. Without all the hassle of rehashing everything they'd had and dragging all their mess out into the open once again. Added bonus—he hadn't quit his job to do this, so he could forget the personal disaster he had and just worry about wildfires.

The idea that he'd wasted his time was like a niggle of doubt against what he'd hoped by taking this job. But was it God's leading or a nudge from elsewhere? Hope for a fresh start without her, or despair and condemnation because she didn't want him in her life?

Maybe he really had come all this way simply so he could see it with his own eyes, be reminded that Tristan and Jamie would always choose each other—even if it hurt them both. Logan could never compete with the bond the siblings had. It could be that God wanted him to consider that part of his past—the Jamie part—as dead. Like his old life.

After all, what had really changed between them since their last conversation?

Just because he was a new man thanks to Jesus, it didn't solve any of the issues he and Jamie might've had before. She would always be determined to save her family whether they appreciated it or not. He would never be able to convince her to let them go.

They needed to get out of here.

Logan would get her to safety, and then he would go back to his team. Do what he'd come up here to do.

Be a smokejumper.

Jamie tried to focus on her brother, but anytime Logan was around, it was like all sense of reason went out the window. She could hardly believe he'd shown up here just in time to rescue her, or that he'd hit that guy over the head.

My hero.

Until he wasn't willing to rescue her anymore because he thought her family wasn't worth saving. Just her. But how could she live with the fact he was willing to help her and not them? As if she were any more valuable than her brother or her mother, or any more deserving of a future.

What they'd had between them might've been great—amazing even. But their problems had no answers, and they'd just gone around and around, unable to reconcile the difference in how they saw things.

She couldn't get sucked into his orbit. Not again.

Even if he was here and had practically straight up told her he wanted another shot, she needed to try and ignore how handsome he still was even years after she'd met him. The guy was going to age well. In thirty years, he'd be a silver-haired fox, and her heart would probably still flutter around him. All that dark hair, and those smoldering eyes trying to trap her. Which was precisely why she needed to focus on her brother and this situation they were in.

Hello, danger. Like, real danger. Not just hot-guy trouble.

This wasn't the time to be distracted. She should be persuading Tristan that staying was a terrible idea so they could *go.*

She turned to her brother. "You could spend *months* trying to work out what they're doing, T. In the end, you'll probably wind up getting arrested as an accomplice."

It wouldn't be a surprise to anyone. Her brother was a good guy with a nasty habit of making poor choices—and the criminal record to prove it. None of it had been in the last few years, except for a few rumors she'd heard about something that'd happened in Benson over the winter. But he was apparently determined to break that streak of being a free man living on the right side of the law.

"I know what I'm doing."

She wanted to believe that. "You should come with us. You don't get points with the law for having nothing to tell them, and that's all you've got so far."

Tristan didn't like hearing that.

"Please, I want to know you're safe." Then she would head back to the Lower 48 and get on with her life—with Tristan there. Safe.

"Logan is here. He will get you out." Her

brother walked to the door. "I'll make sure your path is clear, and then I'll be back when it's time for you to leave."

Logan said nothing, his lips pressed into a thin line.

Jamie turned back to the map. There was always a simplicity in numbers. This string of digits on the side of the map begged her attention, like a puzzle waiting to be solved.

More often than not, she wished people were more like numbers. That the sequence of events or a pattern of behavior made rational sense according to some kind of pre-established equation. But it never worked like that.

Least of all with Logan.

Until things came to a head and he took off. That part was always the same. They reached a stalemate, both realized nothing would ever change, and he left to go fight fires somewhere else.

First Australia.

Now Alaska.

She couldn't believe they'd actually bumped into each other up here.

"Why don't we just make a run for it?" Logan asked. "We don't need to wait for your brother if he isn't coming."

She shook her head, part of her mind puzzling over these numbers.

"Jamie." He touched her shoulder.

"Listen, Logan, I got up here on my own. I'll get back home on my own. I never asked you for help, and you obviously need to get back to your job."

What was the point dragging this out? They weren't supposed to be together, and she *had* been doing just fine without him. Focusing on work. Helping her mom when she needed it. Going to church and . . . When *was* the last time she'd attended Sunday service?

She'd been watching it at her desk most Sundays for a while now.

She should go back to in-person. Get some fellowship. That would help her nurse her again-always-never-healed broken heart once she was back home and trying to forget about Logan.

She should ask Kelsey if she wanted to go out for lunch.

Logan didn't argue with what she'd said, which meant he really *did* need to get to work.

He said, "I'll make sure you're safely out of here. I left my gear by your car. When we get there, we can go our separate ways."

"Better than rehashing it all and realizing we have no more answers than we did two years ago."

If she'd needed help, she would've hired a whole team of protection specialists like Samuel had suggested. She wanted to explain that to

Logan, but she tried not to use her wealth like that in arguments. Her mom and brother sort of knew how much money she made with the company, but aside from her colleagues, not many other people knew who she was at work.

"I'm sure you don't need to worry about Tristan. He's made it this far, and he always seems to land on his feet." His tone was infused with sarcasm. "Even if he's risking getting killed or put in jail every second of the day. How is your mom, by the way? Is she on the wagon, or did she fall off?"

She stared at the map with her teeth clenched. "It wasn't your business before. You didn't care. So why would I tell you now?" She looked at the locations indicated by an X and said, "And if it was Bryce, or your sister Andi who needed your help?"

She was pretty sure they *had* and that he'd come running. It seemed like the twins always showed up for each other. When she and Logan had been dating, she'd appreciated that about their relationship.

How many times had she wished someone would show up for her?

But her family? Apparently they didn't measure up to being worthy of aid.

Logan huffed. "If Bryce kept making bad decisions, there would come a point he'd have to get himself out of the mess. I wouldn't keep bailing him out if it didn't help him. I'd only be prolonging him hitting rock bottom. And that might be *exactly* what he needed."

That's what he thought this was?

Logan had spoken. He'd proclaimed judgment on what her mom and her brother "needed," and his word was law. Just because he believed it, that meant it was true.

Meanwhile, Jamie had fallen into the role of showing up for her family the same way the Crawfords did for each other. They'd all pitched in to help his dad, who'd suffered a TBI after a car accident years ago.

She wanted to be that for her brother and her mom. And what was so wrong with that if she had the resources to do it?

Logan thought she should ditch them and let them fend for themselves. The only reasoning she'd ever figured out for why he believed it was that he thought her family didn't live up to the Crawford standard. Their mom was a high-profile lawyer with big-name clients. Bryce was a lieutenant in the fire department. Andi had married an ATF agent and was working toward being a nurse. They worked hard, held each other to high standards, and always pushed to achieve bigger and better things.

They seemed to forget that other people weren't the same. Some chose to be content where they were rather than push for more or better all the time.

"Someone is outside." Logan turned to put himself between her and the door.

But it was only Tristan.

Jamie moved around her ex and went to her brother, still not willing to let go of the need to bring Tristan out of this with her. Otherwise, what did she have to show for coming up here? "What will it take for you to come with us? What would you need?"

It probably sounded like a business transaction, but she was good at business.

And when all else failed, Jamie fell back on what she knew.

"I told them all I saw you run into the woods," Tristan said. "Everyone tore out after you. ATVs and on foot. They probably took the dogs too."

Jamie shivered. "Then we have time while they're gone. We just need to leave before they return, right?" It was that or draw them away somewhere else.

Logan brushed past them and headed to the door. "Figure it out fast. The guy in the hall is gone."

Tristan said, "They hauled him out."

Jamie needed this conversation back on track. "Tristan, what do you need?"

He scratched a finger on his jaw. "Can you copy all the files on their system?"

"Of course." She could do more than that if she had thirty seconds and internet access.

Logan glanced over at her. Unlike her brother, he probably had no idea what she could do. But then, sharing her work life with him wouldn't have made a difference. Their jobs hadn't been the problem.

Logan said, "What are you, some kind of secret agent now?" He huffed a laugh. "You know they don't hire people with criminal records."

A muscle in Tristan's jaw flexed.

"We need to keep focused, not argue." Jamie could knock their heads together right now. But she'd have to knock hers and Logan's together at the same time. After all, they'd spent some of the last half hour in each other's faces rehashing the past. If they stayed together any longer, the spiral would only continue.

Then they'd *both* hit rock bottom.

"We need to visit the office on the way out." Tristan winced. "But they'll be back soon, and we'll still need some kind of distraction to get away. I can't do that if I'm with you. It's why I'd rather stay here. Play it off like you guys subdued me and ran for it."

She didn't like the sound of that, but at least he was open to coming with them. "We can fake some kind of distraction, right? Get what we need. Meet up and run for it." Sounded easy when she put it like that, but it would likely be far more complicated.

If they worked together, it would be a whole lot easier.

She turned to him. "Logan?"

"I can make a distraction." He looked at Tristan. "I just need some gasoline and a lighter."

FOUR

LOGAN STOMPED HIS FEET ON THE concrete floor, waiting for the right moment. Checking the time on his watch.

He'd found the equipment shed that he'd told Tristan was the best spot for an impromptu blaze. He would hole up in a closet at the back of what was more like a building than a shed, if anyone was going to ask his opinion. But that's what Tristan had called it.

Five minutes to go on the time they'd agreed on, coordinating everything to kick off at the same time so they could run for it in the confusion—which unfortunately wasn't going to be under the cover of darkness.

Since the sun set at midnight and came up again at four a.m., there was zero point in waiting for night that was more like evening dim just so they could make a run for it. It wasn't even lunchtime yet.

His crew would be hard at work cutting the line.

He was here.

Lord, I want to believe this is the right thing. Guide my steps.

Faith didn't mean he had no worries. But he could draw from strength outside himself and pray the three of them would be protected until they got to safety.

He wanted to rush and get them running from here as fast as possible. But haste wasn't always the best way. Sometimes that resulted in more trouble.

Logan checked one more time that the equipment shed was free of anyone nosing around and ducked into the storage closet at the back. Checked his watch again.

Three minutes to go time.

It was the perfect place to set his distraction. At the far end of the compound, the huge equipment building was full of construction machinery, motorcycles in pieces on one side, and small-scale diggers. Even a riding mower and two cordless push mowers. Every kind of tool imaginable was scattered on a workbench cluttered with wrenches, hammers, even a circular saw—and empty beer cans on every spare inch of space.

One wall had two cardboard boxes of newspaper and junk mailers beside at least a cord of wood, in rows and stacked almost all the way to the ceiling, probably for the firepit outside. *Perfect.* There was a roof vent on one side of the apex roof that would allow the smoke to escape and bring in more oxygen for the fire. He would also leave the window open.

He was ready to go. Just one more thing and he'd switch this plan into gear. Logan twisted the dial on his radio and listened to chatter as he turned up the volume.

"Copy that. When you're done, head back." That was Jade.

"Got it, boss." JoJo.

Logan waited for a break in conversation and said, "This is Logan. Does anyone read me?"

"Logan! This is Jade. Where are you?"

Uh-oh. "Still at the camp."

"When are you heading out?"

He said, "I instructed the compound residents to evacuate, but they don't want to listen because the boss won't order it. I'm helping those that do wish to get out of here, but it's taking longer than I thought."

He didn't want to give away everything to anyone who might be listening, but he also wasn't going to lie. The men who'd gone after Jamie, according to Tristan's supposed sighting of her running over the hill, would be back soon enough. If this went to plan, they would rush to this building as soon as they came back into the compound, drawn by the flames from the fire he was about to start.

When he got back to base, he would give Jade and their commander, Tucker Newman, a full briefing so they would know exactly what had happened.

The fact he'd have both Tristan and Jamie to confirm what he told them would help.

Logan said, "I'll be there soon. I'll catch up."

"We're about done with the line," Jade said. "Then we will be heading north to deal with a section of fire that Tucker says looks like it might sweep down and join this one. We'll eat dinner up there tonight. If all is well by evening and the fire is dying down, we'll hike out."

And he was set to go south to Jamie's car while his team headed in the other direction.

Doubling back and going north would take him past the compound again. Logan winced. Would it be better for him to just ride out with Jamie and her brother? "I'll try and get there before dinner. Might take a while though. I have to go back for my gear."

Jade said, "Why's that?"

Of course she asked. "I spotted her car."

They would all know who he was talking about.

Each of them had heard the sob story of how he'd walked away from the woman he loved—loved her then and every day since, if he was honest—and regretted it enough to switch to the Midnight Sun crew when he heard she'd come up here looking for her brother. All for a shot at finding her and convincing her to take a chance on him.

Didn't look like that would happen now, but he'd have to fill everyone in on that as well—the fact that finding her had led to the realization he needed to let her go.

"She's there?" Skye asked, apparently as curious as everyone else. "You found her?"

"I'm helping her, and then I'll hike up. Tell you everything."

His friend said, "Be careful."

Then Jade said, "Keep us posted."

"Thanks. Out." Logan toggled the switch off and left the closet.

A few of the men who occupied this compound had come back. He saw a couple of shadows pass the cloudy glass on the window. The rest were pursuing Jamie, or so they thought, hopefully going far enough up the hill that it would take time to come all the way back. She was safe and sound, tucked away in a closet and working on their computer network. Tristan was . . . wherever Tristan was.

In the meantime, Logan planned to thoroughly distract them.

He needed to draw the militia guys away from the entrance to the compound so he, Jamie, and Tristan could escape in the direction of Jamie's car. Tristan had suggested they grab guns to protect themselves, but the look on Jamie's face had shut that down quick. She didn't want to be in a fight with deadly weapons.

He stacked kindling and wood in a pile in the center of the room, close to the lawnmower side. He opened the gas caps so the fumes floated out. Same with the only intact motorcycle, whether it had gas in it or not. Didn't look like it had worked for a while.

With any luck—or rather, the hand of Providence—he would be able to get a sizeable blaze going in this building.

Logan poured at least a quart from a gas can over the wood and kindling. He flicked on the lighter and fixed it so the flame didn't go out when he let go. Then he tossed it at the blaze and stepped back at the same time.

The gasoline ignited and flames whooshed up toward the ceiling.

Heat filled the room along with the scent of burning fuel. The wood crackled and snapped.

Logan raced over and dragged up a window on the side of the building, then climbed out, praying no one would be hurt by the fire. He left the window open so the fire had access to oxygen that would help it keep burning. He prayed the safeguards these guys had in place—Brian Howards had been right that they were prepared—would keep the fire from spreading to the neighboring building. No one would be injured by the flames.

He also prayed they would be able to do what they needed to do and get out of here.

He ran to the back corner of the building and looked around, toward that cold firepit in the center of the gravel between the structures.

Someone, a male, yelled, "Fire!"

A second later, a guy sprinted toward the front of the equipment shed.

Two guys raced after him. One shoved the other away from him. "Go find Tristan! He's gonna answer for this."

The one ordered to go stumbled but caught himself before he went down. Turned and headed off in the other direction.

Logan waited a second, praying no one would see him race to the office.

Then he sprinted as fast as he could in his boots on the gravel. He skidded to the back door of the office building, a prefab structure that had clearly been trucked up here and then pieced together like a puzzle. He ran in while more shouting erupted outside.

The door clicked shut behind him, and the sound echoed down the empty hall.

Tristan had told him where to find them.

Logan headed for the second door on the right and opened it to a room with metal desks and old computers that should've been upgraded decades ago. A phone sat on a desk, not plugged into anything. Two windows gave him a view of outside through broken blinds. He'd have to be careful not to be seen.

But no Jamie.

Where are you?

Had she and Tristan been forced to hide? Or even to make a run for it without him?

In that moment Logan, was twelve years old again. Sitting on the curb in the dark outside the middle school, waiting to be picked up.

Forgotten.

Jamie shifted in her seat on the floor, aware her legs were going numb. Tristan had told her to hide in the closet. She didn't much care where she was. After all, she'd stayed safe in here long enough to use this laptop he'd found to access the network that connected each computer in this compound via their satellite internet connection.

Logan would be back soon.

She could barely believe he'd found her here in

Alaska. But it wasn't like things would be different this time. All she had to do was focus on getting what Tristan needed so he would leave with her. But the fact she might never let go of what she'd felt for Logan seemed like an old wound that had never healed.

So she pushed aside the hurt and focused on the job.

Jamie had already transferred a hundred thousand dollars from a cryptocurrency account. One that couldn't be traced back to her. It would look like an anonymous donation to this group.

What she couldn't figure out was what they were into. She'd thought drugs at first, or domestic terrorism. A training camp for guys who didn't want to live under federal law. Not unheard of.

But this setup they had in their system connected to . . . something else. She was a finance expert, not a hacker, so she couldn't get past security or firewalls. But money could.

After she'd transferred the money, she started copying all the files to a flash drive she kept in her pack—the backup copy of her files.

As she waited for the transfer to complete, watching that bar slide over to one hundred percent, she went back and checked their account where she'd deposited the money.

She hit enter and refreshed the page.

Frowned.

"Where's the money?" She navigated through pages and found it had been transferred out moments after she'd deposited it. "Not by anyone here. They're all trying to find me." She was careful to keep her voice low just in case someone came into the room. "Who moved my money?"

Someone with access to the bank account on this computer had transferred her hundred thousand dollars out in smaller increments, breaking it up and moving it to other accounts.

Dust tickled her nose, and she scratched it.

With more time, she might be able to follow that money, but the second it was transferred beyond her reach, it would be gone. There was definitely something more happening here. It almost seemed like these people were funded by someone else.

Made to look like an average militia compound in the Alaska backcountry.

Until an investigation dug below the surface.

Jamie sneezed.

She froze, staring at the door. Someone could've heard that. Would it be that guy, Snatch, back with his evil intentions? She shivered.

The handle turned, and a tall man filled the doorway. It took a second for his outfit to register. "Logan."

He held his hand out. "What are you doing in here?"

Jamie let him help her stand, juggling the laptop with her other hand to hug it against her side. "This is where Tristan said to wait for him."

He seemed relieved but also like something else might be bothering him.

She said, "Did the fire go okay?"

He nodded. "Time to go."

"As soon as Tristan gets here."

"How about the files?" He motioned to the computer.

"It's about halfway done copying everything. And get this," she said. "I transferred money into their account, and someone already moved it out."

"What does that mean?"

"I don't know yet." She frowned at the screen. "I need more time to look through all this." Except the minute she left the area, she would lose the connection. Could she find her money later?

It was possible.

With the tracker ring she'd given Tristan, she'd be able to find him too.

The door handle eased down. Jamie touched Logan's sleeve, looking for just a little bit of solidarity. Standing together, side by side, facing what was ahead. Together, the way she'd have said, just a few years ago, that they would be forever.

Right up until the reality of their differences had set in.

Tristan came in. "Ready to go?"

"Yes," Logan said.

Jamie looked at the screen. "I'm done here." She ejected the flash drive and pocketed it, because it was faster than removing her pack and stowing it inside.

The quicker they could get out of here, the faster she'd be able to leave Logan behind as well. Get back to her life in Last Chance County. Her company. Her friends. Things had been going just fine, but this was a good reminder not to hope in things that had no substance.

Too many of her mother's boyfriends had taught her that relationships weren't worth it. She would only get hurt like her mom had over and over again. Jamie had thought Logan might've been different, but this was just more proof that she didn't need to put her heart in danger.

It would only get broken.

"Good. Let's go." Tristan turned to the door . . . and immediately backed up two steps.

A man strode in—an older guy with gray hair and scruff on his face. Jeans and a denim shirt, scuffed boots. He lifted a gun. "Boy, I'm gonna kill—"

Tristan whipped a pistol from his belt and squeezed off a shot.

Blood bloomed on the man's chest, and he fell like a giant tree cut down. He hit the ground with a thud.

Tristan jumped over him. "Come on. Someone will have heard that shot."

Logan tugged Jamie in front of him and didn't let go of her hand. She raced after her brother, still holding the laptop tight to her chest with one arm.

She held on tight to Logan's grip, knowing he would make sure she was safe no matter what happened after they got to her car.

Tristan ran from the back door, across an open space to the fence. "Come on!"

She didn't see a way out. "There's no gate!"

Logan sped up, pulling her along.

Tristan hit the fence, then pulled back a section of the chain link. It bent back, wide enough for her to crawl through on her hands and knees. "Go."

She scrambled up, focusing on that single word. Her brother, with her and not in danger. Safe because she'd come up here to help him.

Go. Jamie glanced back to see men running toward them.

One pointed a pistol, firing wildly.

She gasped. "Watch out!"

Logan was already through. He tugged her arm. "Come on. We need to get to those trees."

She didn't know what they were, all clustered together. Almost like skinny Christmas trees. It would probably be dark at ground level, or close to it. A great place to hide—or run as fast and as far as they could. "Come on, T!"

Jamie didn't have the words to say a prayer. She would rather drag her brother along the way Logan was doing with her.

But Tristan caught up to her side, and it seemed like her aerobic ability—or lack thereof—might be slowing *them* down.

If she didn't pick up some speed, they might all get shot.

Logan headed between two trees ahead of them, Tristan behind Jamie. She stumbled on an uneven patch of ground and went down. She managed to hold on to the laptop and planted her other hand in pine needles. Logan wound an arm around her, but she got her feet under her, and he didn't need to carry her. She wasn't going to slow them down.

"I'm okay," Jamie said.

But Logan wasn't looking at her.

A gunshot cracked behind them. He dived at her, and her back hit the ground as Logan landed on top of her, shielding her with his body, smelling like sweat and . . . man. Maybe the scent was just inherently Logan, because she'd never been attracted to a guy's smell before.

Tristan crouched by a tree. "I'll hold them off."

Her brother turned and fired at the gunmen. Risking his own life to protect theirs.

Logan hauled her up for a second time. "Come on." Before she could argue, Logan added, "Tristan, you'd better be behind us."

Her brother only said, "Go!"

Jamie grabbed the laptop, and Logan pulled her deeper into the forest. She ran until her legs screamed and her chest hurt. When she glanced back to see if Tristan or either of the gunmen were on their tails, she spotted a dark, wet stain on the side of Logan's shirt.

Jamie gasped. "You've been shot!"

FIVE

I T DOESN'T MATTER." LOGAN TURNED away from her so she couldn't see his wound. Given how it felt, he doubted it was worse than a graze. Then again, she wasn't exactly wrong that he had been shot. "We need to get out of here."

She stared at him, all wide eyes and mussed hair. Both arms around that laptop. Was she in shock?

Logan touched her elbow and eased her away from the compound behind them. "Come on. We need to keep moving."

They'd run a ways from where he'd dived on her. Hopefully Tristan was holding off the gunmen who had been chasing them. Unless they needed him alive for some reason, he was putting himself at risk. To save them.

Probably more like to save his sister. Logan wasn't sure Tristan cared about him all that much.

But either way, his actions had enabled them to make a run for it to safety.

"Is he going to be okay?"

Logan prayed her brother would be, but that was all he could do. Right now, his priority was getting Jamie to safety. "He knows how to survive if he got this far. And he wanted to take the information you have from the compound. That means you and I don't get captured and taken back there or it was all for nothing. So, in order to do what Tristan wanted, we have to keep going. We have to get the files away from here."

But what did Tristan intend to do with them?

For all Logan knew, he was planning to sell information to Brian Howards' enemies for cash so he could fund whatever he planned to do next.

Hopefully, Jamie would see the logic in handing whatever it was over to the police instead of back to her brother the next time she saw him.

She glanced over her shoulder, but they kept going. Rather than take the same deer trail he had taken to get to the compound, Logan skirted the edge of the trees and chose a roundabout route back to the car. It took longer, and his side stung. He could feel that the blood had soaked his shirt more than before.

Logan didn't want to stop. He wanted to keep

going, get in the car and drive out of here. But pretty soon, blood loss would make his head start to swim.

Then he would be the one in shock. And he didn't need both of them in more trouble than they already were.

He did a mental inventory of everything he had on his person, which apparently no longer included the radio. Must've dropped it.

Jamie glanced back over her shoulder.

Logan dug into the thigh pocket of his cargoes and pulled out a flat, square packet.

"There's a lot more blood on your shirt than before." She came toward him and took the packet. "What is this?"

"It's basically just gauze, but it has this powder stuff on it that stops the bleeding. Mostly they use it in military settings. It could save a life in the moment when something nasty happens."

"Well, even if your life isn't in imminent danger, we're still going to use it on you." She tore open the packet. "Lift up your shirt."

Logan grinned. "I thought you'd never ask."

"This isn't the time to make light of what's happening."

"Sorry." He winced, and not only because she helped him peel the material of his shirt away from the wound.

"This is a pretty nasty graze."

"Stings."

She pressed the gauze against the wound. "It doesn't cover all of it. You need two."

"Only got one." He let out a breath and lowered his shirt, keeping his hand over the gauze now stuck to his wound. She looked up at him, and he saw the worry in her eyes. "I'm sure Tristan is going to be okay."

"I put a tracking device on him."

Logan blinked. "You did what?"

"It's this ring thing. I slipped it into his pocket the first time I saw him. It's new tech. They're looking for backers, and my company is going to fund it."

"What do you mean 'your company'?" Before, when she talked about work, she'd always said "the company I work for." But not this time. "Did you start a business? That's impressive."

She shook her head. "I still work at the same place."

Huh. Maybe they were both just miscommunicating. "We should keep walking."

Jamie looked around. "Where are we even going? I mean, at least those guys have stopped chasing us. But still."

He touched her back and rubbed a hand between her shoulder blades. "All we can do is keep praying for Tristan."

She didn't respond to that.

They set off walking, falling into a comfortable silence. Or more likely, a stalemate. For a while, they found a trail. After that, he had her take a more direct route through the brush where it thinned out, and they were able to pick through the wilds.

Jamie said, "Do you have some kind of GPS that tells you where to go? Because I'm completely lost."

"There's a compass in my pack, but I left it with my stuff at your car." Felt like days ago now that he'd been so surprised to see a vehicle with her stuff in it. So much had happened since then that it really should be dark by now, even with the long Alaska day. And yet it had barely been a few hours.

"So how do you know where we're going?"

He looked up at the sky. "The position of the sun. The direction we walked and the hill to the right, the one we're skirting around. I'll admit, we're going the long way on purpose so that we don't run into those guys. They'll probably expect us to take the trail that's most direct to get to your car as fast as possible."

Jamie kept walking ahead of him. "Doesn't that mean they'll be waiting at the car when we get there?"

"If they are, then we'll just have to leave your car and keep walking." He thought he might have heard her groan but wasn't sure. Maybe he needed to distract her, but all he had in his head was the need to get her to safety.

Even though he'd decided to walk away from her as soon as she was all right, that didn't mean he would ever quit caring about what happened to her.

Logan said, "A couple of months ago, before I came up here, we were training before the start of the wildfire season. I got a call from my sister that Bryce had disappeared, that he might've been kidnapped. For hours I had no idea if he was all right or even alive. All I knew was that he was gone and no one knew where to find him."

Jamie glanced at him over her shoulder. "Do you get that twin thing where you can feel each other's pain?"

"It's more complicated than that," he said. "It's usually not physical. It's more of an impression of what he's feeling. Or at least, I know there's no reason I should be feeling anxious or sad or scared. Or happy."

"Did you know he was in trouble?"

Logan said, "I had to walk away from the Ember base camp so I could take a minute and just breathe through his anxiety."

He'd tried to call Bryce but there was no answer. Then he'd tried his sister. His mom. None of his family had known where to find his brother.

He'd even called the Last Chance County Fire Department chief at Bryce's firehouse, but Macon hadn't known where to find him either.

"All I could do for him was pray."

She kept her attention on the path in front of them, picking her way between the trees. The terrain now angled down and to the left, thankfully not sharply. They would be near the car soon enough.

"I had to let go and let God be in control of what happened to Bryce because even if I'd left Montana, I would never have gotten to Last Chance County in time. Even if it made me feel a little bit like I'd been left out—left behind—again." He shrugged. "But that's my issue."

He had friends, and friends of friends, who had access to helicopters and airplanes. Still, by the time he'd considered making that decision, he'd found out Bryce was okay. Bryce had texted him later that day and said he was all right. Bryce had called later and told him all about the governor's chief of staff and the case Penny—the woman his brother had been hung up on for a while—had been working.

They'd chatted later that night, and his brother had filled him in on everything. Including that he was in love. Maybe everyone just assumed someone else had called him to tell him his twin brother was safe—that he and Penny were both out of danger. But while no one had updated him after Bryce was found, his brother at least had touched base. Connected.

"So you came up to Alaska? You're even farther away now," she said. "Why not just work closer to home? That way you can be nearby in case something happens to your family."

"Turns out I had a reason to be here." Logan didn't know if he was ready to rehash the fact that he'd told her he wanted her back. Given he'd changed his mind because they would never agree on the way she bailed out her family constantly, what was the point?

He strode by her on her left side, where the tree line ended. Below them stretched miles of land as far as he could see. Great mountain peaks and snowcapped Denali. So much green below the wide blue sky spotted with clouds. Only a thin trail of smoke obscured the scenery, since the fire was mostly behind them.

"I would have missed this."

She didn't have to know he was also talking about her.

Considering her brother could be in mortal danger, Jamie was trying not to begrudge Tristan the fact he'd come all the way up to Alaska. Given the fact Logan was also here, maybe it wasn't such a stretch for someone to decide they wanted to spend time in this remote, isolated part of America.

She might not feel the same need to save Logan if he got into trouble as she did with her little brother, but that didn't mean she would ever quit caring what happened to him. He was simply far more able to take care of himself.

The only thing she had to distract her from the spiral of being frustrated with everyone and their choices was something Logan had said. That he'd prayed for his brother.

Jamie glanced at him, now walking beside her. "So . . . you pray now?"

She had been the only believer when they'd dated before. Not a dealbreaker for her, although some people certainly thought it should be. Plenty of older ladies at church had frowned at her. As if falling in love with a good man, a hero in the community, was a bad thing.

Maybe that was part of the reason she hadn't gone in person for a long time.

Logan nodded, still walking with one hand over the bloodied part of his shirt. He hadn't said anything about the pain he was surely in. As soon as they got back to the car, she could give him some ibuprofen at least.

He said, "After what happened to Andi a couple of years ago, Bryce and I both started talking about faith. Her husband Jude shared about the Bible with us and explained what it means to be a Christian. It just made sense. We went to a service, and we both prayed at the same time."

Jamie couldn't remember the day she had given her life to Christ. Some kind of children's service decades ago, where she'd been told to ask Jesus into her heart.

"That's amazing." Because it was. Even if he'd been a good person before, the fact he lived as a Christian now meant he always had someone to rely on. A place to go for strength, wisdom, and true joy.

When was the last time she had any of those things?

He said, "It definitely hasn't been easy, and I feel like I'm still learning a lot. But there are a few people with the Midnight Sun Wildland Firefighters who also are believers, so we have a little Bible study going on our days off."

It sounded like a lot of things had changed since they'd broken up. And not all on his side, given she had realized how far away she felt from God.

If she had listened to God or even asked for His opinion before she'd come up here, things might have gone a lot differently. Logan might not have been grazed by a bullet.

Tristan could be dead now, for all she knew.

Tears gathered in her eyes. Jamie blinked them back, trying not to give in to the sting of realizing she was responsible for a lot of what had happened today. "We should pray for Tristan."

Logan glanced over, nodded. "I've been doing that since the last time we saw him. And if he has one of those trackers you mentioned, then maybe you can find him once we get somewhere you can connect to the internet on that laptop."

She had her own laptop as well, in the duffel in her car. Along with her phone. All she needed to do was call Samuel and admit what'd happened, and he would find Tristan from his computer. But she didn't exactly want to talk to her number two guy at the company right now when she could barely keep her emotions in check.

"I see your car."

She looked where he indicated and could see part of the side and the red paint of her rental. Same color as her car at home. Something she'd thought was a good sign, or at least a way to find it easily out here.

Thank You. God certainly could have had a hand in that, and it was past time for Jamie to renew her faith in Him.

"Keys?" He approached the car cautiously.

She didn't see any gunmen. Couldn't hear anyone tromping around the woods—except her and Logan. But if someone were hiding and waiting for them to emerge? She and Logan would be shot before they realized what was happening.

Cold washed over her, and she shivered.

Logan stepped closer to her, touching her cheek. "Almost there. You just need to hang on a little longer and we'll get to safety."

She nodded, determined to do this herself. She didn't want to rely on a guy she couldn't even agree with. Except about faith, apparently. The way she stuck her neck out for her family would always be the thing between them. Even though that was exactly what he did with his family, always showing up for them. Or praying until he knew they were safe when he was too far away to pitch in.

When she did that, it was apparently the wrong thing to do. Because some people had more value. Or they were more deserving of help than others.

At least, as far as he thought.

Jamie slid the backpack from her shoulders and dug out her keys, handing them to him. If he wanted to go over there first, then he could put himself in danger. She hung back, waiting while he beeped the locks and checked around the car.

"We're good."

She headed for the car, but he slipped in the front seat before she even reached it. She muttered to herself, "I guess you're driving." She pulled open the passenger side door and got in.

"Can you get us out of here when you have a bullet wound on your side?"

"I'm good." He didn't waste any time, spraying gravel as he made the turn to go down the fire road that would take them to the blacktop asphalt street at the bottom of the hill. "How did you even know where to come?"

"I asked around town and at the Midnight Sun Saloon over a period of weeks, all to find out who he was hanging with. Even though Sheriff Starr had no idea how I could find my brother, there were enough people in town who had seen him. They warned me off though. Told me to leave it be because those guys are dangerous. Finally I tracked down someone who knew about the militia guys he came to town with, and they knew where to find this place. There was a guy who wrote down all the directions and got me where I wanted to go."

Logan held the wheel with one hand, his jaw tight.

Whether he liked it or not, she had done what she felt she needed to. As long as Tristan got out, then what was the problem? Jamie glanced out the back window. "Maybe we should wait and see if he comes after us."

She spotted his stuff piled on her back seat. Smokejumper gear.

Logan said, "Gotta get you to safety, and then

I need to meet up with my team. Do the job I'm being paid for."

More likely he needed medical treatment, but she wasn't going to argue with him right now. Maybe smokejumpers just had a different way of doing things and she wasn't used to it because she worked from home and called into the office whenever needed.

"Sorry I'm keeping you from your duties."

He let go some of the tension, enough to reach over and squeeze her knee. "It was important."

It seemed like he would drop her as soon as it was done, the way he always did. Leave and go somewhere else. *He* might be different now, but it seemed like their circumstances hadn't changed.

Never would.

Logan said, "Make sure you talk to the sheriff before you leave town. Tell him everything you know about that compound and the guys we met up here. The sheriff will need both of our stories."

"Of course I'm going to talk to the sheriff. But I'm not leaving town until I know Tristan is safe. He's the whole reason I came up here."

"Sheriff Starr and his people can make sure your brother is okay." Logan glanced over at her, then continued down the rutted dirt road.

She glanced in the side mirror but couldn't see anyone following them. Not even Tristan. Had leaving him behind really been the right thing to do? Maybe for them.

Probably not for Tristan.

Logan said, "It's probably for the best if you just go back to Last Chance County."

SIX

AN HOUR LATER, THERE WAS ENOUGH signal on the cell phone stuffed in Jamie's duffel that Logan was able to use it to contact base camp. Next time he went out, he was bringing his cell phone with him.

The phone rang against his ear and finally connected. "Midnight Sun base camp. This is Commander Newman."

Logan had called all the way through to the commander's desk phone. No point going up the chain when he could go straight to the source. "It's Logan Crawford."

"Good to hear from you. Jade called in a little while back pretty worried about where you were."

Logan winced, one hand on the wheel and the other holding the phone to his ear. "I'm good. I'm driving Jamie back to town."

"Bring her back to base camp."

Despite being commander, Tucker Newman didn't normally bark out orders like that. Logan didn't like the sound of it. "Um, sir?"

"You heard me. Get that girl back to base camp. The rest of your team will be in tonight, so there's no point catching up with them just to turn around and come back to base."

"They got the fire under control?" Jade had told him they were going to check out another one.

"A team from up north came down and took care of part of it. I sent one of the drivers out with the bus to pick them up."

"Copy that, Commander."

Tucker hung up. Logan handed the phone back to Jamie. "Thanks."

"Everything okay?"

She hadn't said much to him since he'd made that comment about her going back to Last Chance County. He didn't know why, considering that was where she lived. It was where she'd come from. Her brother had proven he could land on his own two feet and would continue to take care of himself. The guy had always been scrappy and street smart. That wouldn't change just because Tristan was up in Alaska, elbow-deep in whatever those backwoods guys were up to.

"Sure. Everything's fine." Logan headed in the

general direction of where Tucker had ordered him to go. "Can you type an address into the GPS? We're headed back to base camp."

"Where all the hotshots and smokejumpers live?"

Logan nodded. "It's pretty remote, but that's not surprising up here."

He gave her the information, and she got her phone going, plugged into the charger. "I downloaded a lot of the maps of the area while I had signal, just in case I hit a spot with no service."

"Smart." The car, connected to her phone, beeped with a couple of notifications. Incoming emails the car wanted to read aloud to her.

Jamie dismissed the notifications.

Logan glanced over. "Work stuff?" When they got back to base camp, she would be able to check in with her company. They had surprisingly good internet.

"Probably just worried about me and looking for an update on Tristan."

"You told the people you work with about your brother?"

She shrugged. "And my mom and how she's doing well right now. She's in this rehab place I found just outside Benson, in Washington. They care about my family."

"That's great." He didn't want his voice to sound tight, as if he were begrudging them success. Her mom had struggled with addiction to both drugs and alcohol for years. If she was doing better and working to fight back, that wasn't a bad thing.

One of the guys on the hotshot team in Montana had been a SWAT officer in Benson. He had overcome a pain-pill addiction, and faith had strengthened him in the fight for recovery. Logan hadn't known the guy before he got clean, found Jesus, and decided to be a wildland firefighter. He couldn't even imagine who Dakota had been before.

One day, someone would be able to say the same thing about Jamie's mom. That in knowing who she had become, they couldn't even imagine who she had been before.

The way they'd say that about the difference in his life.

"Change is good," he said. "And growth. I've bumped into a few people I used to know before I found Christ, and they barely recognize how I act now compared to who I was."

They fell into a comfortable silence, and he almost forgot the nagging, stinging pain in his side. Right up until he had to fight with the steering wheel to get from the asphalt road onto the dirt that led up to the Midnight Sun base camp.

Grass grew on either side of the road, cut short by one of the guys who worked in the office. Every time he felt cooped up, he jumped on his riding lawnmower and mowed down an acre or two. Logan didn't blame the guy. He would much rather be outside than indoors, especially during wildfire season.

He crested the hill and Jamie gasped.

Probably because she could see the expanse of the base camp, nestled between the river and the bottom of the hills that flanked the far side of the runway and protected them from the wind.

Likely not because of the eight hotshots jogging up the road in front of them.

"This place is huge."

Logan loved every square foot of it. "The runway has been here for years, and a few of the older buildings. You can see the Quonset huts between the aircraft hangars on the far side. Those are original, as is the one office building on the east side."

"What about the rest of the structures and those log buildings on the south side?"

"Four of the guys, they usually go by 'the Trouble Boys,' and one of the women—she's always hanging with them—came up from Montana before winter."

"The Trouble Boys?"

"Don't ask me why we started calling them that," Logan said. "They're great people."

She leaned forward to peer out the window.

"Anyway," Logan said, "they started building cabins on one side of the runway before the winter hit and got it all done quick enough that they spent the cold months doing all the interior work, totally tricking out all the kitchens and bathrooms. We have a huge residence cabin for the guys, another one for the girls, both of which have huge living areas and entertainment rooms. The one in the middle is a cabin for married couples. It has suites, so each couple has a living room and bedroom and their own bathroom."

"Wow. It's impressive."

Logan slowed the car. He rolled down his window as he approached the two men at the back of the pack of joggers running down to base camp. Mitch Bronson was the hotshot crew chief, and beside him ran a huge guy with an overgrown beard—Grizz. No one knew what his first name was.

Logan lifted two fingers and Grizz nodded.

Neither Mitch nor Grizz was sweating, even though they were running a decent pace. They were just bringing up the rear. Keeping an eye on everyone else.

Logan told Jamie who they were. Mitch leaned forward and waved at her through the window. "Mitch came up from Cal Fire a few years ago. He's great. The kind of guy with an even temperament, who everyone respects because he's been doing this for years."

He kept driving and approached the young-est hotshot, Mack. Hammer's younger brother ran beside Sanchez—the girl who hung with the Trouble Boys. The two of them couldn't have been more different, though they both had dark hair. Mack grinned at something Sanchez said.

"Hey, guys." Logan eased off the gas pedal a little more. "Need a ride?"

"Not on your life." Sanchez started running faster, almost racing the car. Mack sprinted and caught up with her, and the two of them passed Raine, who was an Alaskan native. A local. She shook her head at them as they sped by her and Hammer.

Logan slowed. "I won't offer you guys a ride." Instead, he said, "This is Jamie."

Raine glanced over, her gait slowing as she peeked in the window to get a look at his pas-senger. "When we get back, I want to hear what happened."

Logan kept on rolling down the dirt road.

Jamie said, "Is it just me, or does she know who I am?"

He didn't exactly want to admit he'd men-tioned her. "Two more hotshots and that's the whole crew."

Sanchez and Mack had caught up to the last two guys, one with Middle Eastern coloring and his hair pulled back in a bun. The other was Kane, who tended to be quiet and kept his attention more on Sanchez than on fire. Logan had known them for more than a year and had never seen Kane and Sanchez act like more than friends, but what did he know?

He introduced them to Jamie and then left them to finish their run while he drove slowly. He didn't want to kick up dirt behind the car that the others would have to breathe in on the last mile down to base camp.

They passed the wood sign that said "Midnight Sun Wildland Firefighter Base."

Finding a parking space took him a couple of laps around the lot, but he managed to squeeze in beside Mack's vintage motorcycle and the lifted truck covered in dirt that belonged to Mitch.

"Come on, I'll show you to the office and introduce you to Commander Newman." Logan shut his door and reached in the back for his smoke-jumper gear. *Ouch.* "Actually, I probably need to get checked out by the medic."

"Afterward, will you show me around?"

Logan nodded. "Of course." He figured he would need the fresh air after Tucker tore him a new one for getting involved with local gunmen.

She switched out some things between her pack and her duffel and swung the pack over her shoulder. "Need help carrying anything?"

Logan shook his head.

"Just in case I didn't say it before..." She looked almost nervous, staring at him over the roof of the car. "Thanks for coming in there to get me."

"You're welcome, Jamie."

At one time he'd thought he would spend the rest of his life with her.

But now it was time to let her go.

Half an hour later, after she'd told Tucker Newman all about the compound and her brother and he'd put in a call to the sheriff, Jamie was finally alone. Tucker's assistant had gone home for the day so she could pick up her kids from school, and the commander had sequestered himself back in his office off to the side.

Leaving her alone in the open area.

She sat in the waiting-room-style chair and tugged out her laptop, leaving the one from the compound in her bag. She used her personal device to get on the Wi-Fi and sent an email to Samuel, updating him on everything that'd happened. She asked him to run GPS on the ring she'd slipped in Tristan's pocket.

Once she was done and the email was sent, the clarity of focus passed. Everything rushed back, so many things vying for the forefront of her mind. Most of them centered around Logan and what they had been through today.

Her stomach rumbled. They'd given her coffee, but it had long since worn off.

Two women appeared in the open doorway.

"There you are," the brunette with the short hair said. "I'm Raine, and this is Sanchez. Maybe you don't remember. I'm terrible with names."

Jamie said, "I remember you guys."

Taking the time to introduce all of them to her as they passed had been such a typically Logan thing to do when he expected her to leave at the first available moment and go back down to Last Chance County.

He didn't mean for her to connect with the people who lived here. He definitely wasn't expecting her to want to stay and hang out with new friends. He was just so unflinchingly polite.

Sanchez looked her up and down. "So *you're* Jamie."

Jamie frowned. "What's that supposed to mean?"

Raine turned to glare at her friend. "Sanchez, we were trying to be cool about it."

Raine looked back at Jamie. "Logan told us you might want a tour of the jump base. Dinner should be ready in an hour, and the smokejumpers will be back by then as well. Things will get busy."

It hadn't occurred to Jamie until now that she was probably staying overnight. Logan didn't want to show her around, even though she'd asked him for a tour. Most likely he wanted to maintain his distance until she left. "I had a hotel room in Copper Mountain. I guess I'm not going to make it back there tonight."

Raine tipped her head to the side. "I can have someone grab your stuff for you and bring it over if you want."

That meant Jamie probably needed to check out of the hotel. Things were so up in the air right now. She stood. "You know what? I would love a tour."

Even with all the walking they'd done this morning, she had been sitting for a while.

Sanchez held out her hand. "I'll carry your backpack."

Raine glanced at Jamie. "She was in the military or something. We don't ask. We've just learned it's best not to argue."

"Okay then." Jamie handed it over, and Sanchez slipped the straps onto her shoulders.

The girls led Jamie to the same stairwell she'd ascended to get up to the commander's office, from which he could watch out the window as aircraft landed or took off from the base. While she'd been talking to him, a plane had landed that he'd told her carried foam retardant they sprayed on fires. He'd gotten on the radio and added some information about windspeed that'd helped the pilot land safely.

"Is it just me, or do you guys seem to know who I am?"

Sanchez, in the lead, didn't turn around.

These women didn't look like what Jamie would have thought firefighters would look like. But then, one of the fire lieutenants in Last Chance County was a blonde, so maybe she was just making sweeping generalizations. Even if they were girly, they were also clearly strong women who went up against the guys as equals.

Raine said, "Everyone knows Logan only came up here because of a girl. Some of the crew were at the Jude County base in Ember, Montana, last summer, so they know him pretty well."

Raine probably had all the guys fighting over her at the Midnight Sun Saloon whenever they went into town. Her short brown hair was curly and messy and framed her face. "I got the feeling they were all pretty surprised to see Logan when he jumped on one of the open spots right before rookie elimination started."

"When was that? Because I've been up here a couple of months." If Logan had come up here because of a girl, Jamie didn't want to bump into her and have to make awkward conversation. Maybe that was why he'd fallen back on politeness the second they'd gotten near the base. "Looking for my brother, Tristan."

Probably by now, they'd all heard the story.

Sanchez stopped at the door. "He came up here looking for you."

Jamie frowned.

"He knew you were up here looking for your brother."

"Yeah, there's no confusion over his opinion on that." Jamie didn't really want to talk about it. Logan had told her exactly how he felt about her brother, and nothing had changed since they broke up the last time.

"It's pretty romantic if you ask me," Raine said. "Dropping everything and coming up here to find you." She flinched. "Oh! You should make him mac and cheese!"

Sanchez just stared at her.

Raine was about to say something else, but her phone distracted her. She moved a couple of steps away, talking on her cell phone to someone about hotels in Copper Mountain.

Jamie said, "You were going to show me around?"

Sanchez nodded. "Come on."

Jamie stepped out, wincing against the sun, high in the sky. She trotted a couple of steps to catch up with them and slid her sunglasses out of the side pocket of her backpack. Much better.

Sanchez said, "This is the south side of the runway. Everything over by the mountains is the north side. The office is at one end, closest to the entrance. The top level is an observation room with a huge living area, if you want to get away from everyone and sit somewhere quiet. Parking is beside the office." She paused barely long enough to take a breath. "We have one passenger plane for the smokejumpers, one retardant plane, and two choppers—one of which does water drops."

"You sound like the promotional brochure." Raine jogged to catch up with them. "Did we ask her about Logan?"

Sanchez just stared at Raine, then looked at Jamie. "On this side of the runway, we have three cabins around a central firepit. Beyond them is an area where you can park an RV or trailer, if you have one."

Jamie said, "Logan told me there's a women's cabin and a men's one. And one for couples."

Raine nodded. "That's the middle cabin. Ours is the closest one."

Sanchez led them between the runway and the cabins, walking toward the sun that was still high in the sky even though it was after six in the evening. "You can see the hangars on the far side of the runway. Each plane gets its own. There's a helicopter hangar on the right and two helicopter landing pads next to it. Behind the hangars we have a vehicle depot where they keep ATVs and the pushback vehicles that bring airplanes in and out of the hangars. Next to it—behind the hangars—we have a couple of Quonset huts no one really uses anymore. They're pretty grimy."

In contrast, the cabins looked brand-new. "Did you really build the cabins over the winter?"

Sanchez shrugged. "Can't do much outside with all the snow, but we got the exteriors done before it really hit heavy, and then we just focused on inside."

Raine said, "It was pretty impressive to watch. But I'm not complaining, since the Quonset huts were gross, and I was about to say something if we had to live another season in them. Although I don't think anyone realized that the cabins are on the opposite side of the runway from the mess hall."

She pointed to a building down the road beyond the hangars. At the end of that road there was another hangar with the doors rolled up. Someone drove a forklift out of the building, in a circle, and then back inside.

"It seems like a great setup."

Raine grinned. "Us girls are all close. We share everything. Even socks."

Sanchez shot her a look. "You're the one who's been borrowing my socks!"

Raine dissolved into giggles, though Sanchez

didn't seem to find it quite as funny. She led them to the women's cabin, where a row of plastic Adirondack chairs lined the porch. Most had a blanket on top. A mug and a worn Bible had been left on a small round table between two of the chairs.

The girls headed inside, and Jamie turned to look one more time at the Midnight Sun jump base. Hangars. Buildings that looked like they'd been here for years, weathering the elements Alaska threw at them. She saw a brown dog with long curly hair dart out of the mess hall building door and run into the hangar beside it.

No matter the warmth she'd found with these women, who seemed intent on inviting her into their lives, she was still worried about Tristan. Her brother was the reason she'd come up here.

Not Logan and the community he'd found.

A school bus pulled between the cabin and the office where she had spoken with Commander Newman. It turned left and drove in front of the cabins, where the driver parked on the asphalt between the firepit and the runway. A line of bedraggled-looking smokejumpers filed out, dispersing to the three cabins. Logan's crew.

People who looked out for each other and watched each others' backs.

Meanwhile, Jamie had never had anyone who showed up for her the way these people would for their team.

At least, not until Logan.

The bus pulled away, and she saw Logan walking across the runway toward them. A female smokejumper with brown hair, probably early twenties, trudged past Jamie and went into the cabin.

Jamie couldn't tear her gaze from Logan.

She wouldn't come up to Alaska for anything other than someone she cared about. That was why she'd done what she had to do and shown up to go after her brother.

Had he really come up here to find her? The girls seemed to be convinced it was true. But despite him originally saying he thought they should try and get back together, his actions and his words now painted a different picture, and she couldn't get a clear image.

All Jamie knew?

She didn't want to leave before she figured it out.

SEVEN

LOGAN LOOKED OUT THE WINDOW of the single men's cabin, wondering what Jamie thought of the base. It was huge—but Alaska made everything look bigger. Then he wondered why he cared what she thought, considering she would be leaving first thing in the morning.

Kane slapped him on the shoulder. "Relax. The girls will take care of her."

"Right. I'm sure she's fine." They probably all figured he'd sneak out and visit her in the girls' living room later, but they didn't have to know that wasn't going to happen. Only Orion would be aware he didn't leave their shared room.

In the corner of the guys' living area, in lieu of a dining table, they had dragged in a pool table they'd got from a bar in Anchorage that had closed down. Saxon was playing pool with Hammer and Mack. Vince and Orion were chatting by the fridge, close to where Grizz stirred a pot on the stove, his big meaty fist grasping the handle of the wooden spoon.

Logan bellied up to the other side of the breakfast bar. He had to hand it to the Trouble Boys—they'd definitely designed the space with its use in mind. Even though there were eight guys in the room, it didn't feel crowded. He said, "What's for dinner?"

Grizz kept stirring, all his focus on the pot. "How should I know? This is for Jubal."

Vince glanced over, breaking off his conversation with Orion. "Grizz thinks the dog has a sensitive stomach."

"So you either don't care or you're just blind."

Vince shot the big man a look. "Speak for yourself."

"Just because Cadee isn't here, doesn't mean you need to pick a fight with me. Go find your girlfriend if you want to bicker with someone." Grizz shut off the burner and moved the pot to the other side of the stove.

Vince looked like he wanted to say something, but Orion shoved him out of the kitchen. Always the peacemaker. But then he said to Logan, "So, you found her."

Logan had figured they would get around to

asking him about Jamie sooner or later. He just never thought it would be Orion asking—at least, not outside their shared room. The guy was also a believer, which made them a good match to double up in one of the rooms with twin beds.

Grizz didn't share with anyone. Neither did Vince, which wasn't surprising. Saxon and Kane shared a room, and Hammer and his little brother Mack doubled up next door. Mitch, the hotshot boss, lived in an old Airstream on the side of the cabins.

But they still all had to coexist in the open-plan living space. Where they now all started to crowd around. Waiting for the juicy story?

Logan sighed. "Yes, I found her."

Vince said, "No surprise, since you didn't show up to help us cut the line."

He wasn't quite sure what that dig at his actions meant. Probably just that it had never happened before. "Don't worry, it won't happen again."

He could tell Orion had something he wanted to say. Hopefully the guy would leave it for when no one else was around.

The intercom speaker by the front door buzzed.

Vince headed for the door. "Chow time."

The rest of them filed out after him, leaving Orion and Logan to cross the runway together. The girls came out of their cabin and headed for the mess hall as well. Logan spotted Jamie among them, chatting with Jade.

That was good. Logan liked Jade and her boyfriend, Crispin, who was always close by. Not that it was easy to find him. Jade and Skye both reminded him a lot of his sister Andi, back in Last Chance County.

Orion said, "Did she find her brother?"

"We had to leave him behind. But the sheriff can locate Tristan and make sure he's safe."

"Isn't that what Jamie came here to do?"

"She should be going back to her life. Tangling with these guys isn't something she needs to do." Which he would have told her if she'd let him in on her plan to come up here. In fact, if she'd talked to him at all about finding Tristan, Logan would probably have come up here on his own, just like she had. He'd have offered to find the guy for her.

But they hadn't spoken to each other in over a year.

Until Bryce told him he'd heard she was coming up here to look for Tristan, Logan had been trying not to even think about her.

"Isn't going all out for family a good thing?" Orion said. "I mean, who wouldn't want a woman who never gives up? Never surrenders."

"Did you just quote a sci-fi movie to me?"

"Yeah, because it's the best one ever."

"I thought you were all about *Trek of the Os-*

prey." The guys had been binging it in their time off since the locals in the crew here had discovered everyone who'd come up from Montana knew Spenser Storm. They all wanted to invite him up to Alaska for the end-of-season party.

"TV. Movies. Sci-fi is a good distraction from real life."

"I prefer to stay below the clouds."

Maybe that was what he'd been enjoying about being single. For the eight months he'd been with Jamie, it had always seemed like he was spinning out. Trying to keep up with her attempts to rescue her family. The first time they'd broken it off, he'd gone to Australia for a while with Macon. After his buddy had persuaded him to come home, there had been all that stuff with the Sosa cartel and his brother-in-law Jude. Things never seemed to calm down before something else kicked off and things went crazy.

Unless he was in the sky with a parachute above him and nothing but air between him and the ground.

When all he could think about was steering in the right direction, and praying God sent the right air currents to help him along.

This morning, God had dropped Logan right in the path of Jamie. He could now say he'd done exactly what he'd come up here to do, and it turned out it had all been so he could figure out it was time to let her go.

Logan said, "Anyway, what's so bad about your life you need to escape into entertainment?" He hadn't noticed anything wrong with Orion. Or preoccupying him. "Is something going on?"

Orion shrugged. The guy was young enough he'd only qualified as a smokejumper this year, though he'd gotten a jump on the whole wildland firefighting thing because his mom ran a teens camp in Montana called Wildlands Academy that taught firefighting skills.

Last summer, Orion had met his father for the first time. Charlie, a colleague of Logan's from the Last Chance County Fire Department, hadn't even known he had a son. After working with Charlie for a couple of months, Orion had put it together that he was the result of a teenage fling between Charlie and Jayne, his mom.

"Whatever it is, God's got it, right?"

Orion nodded. "That's right. And it's why I feel like I should tell you not to discount Jamie and the real reason she might be here. Seems like something happened while you were out there."

Logan shrugged. "Pretty sure I realized whatever was between us isn't worth it now. Nothing's changed."

"You're different than you were when you guys

dated before. But that's not really what I'm talking about. Maybe God directed you both up here."

Logan had prayed that God would lead him. He didn't know if Jamie had done the same thing, but he wanted to live a life where the Lord directed his steps. "If we still have the same obstacles between us, what's the point? Besides, I live up here now, and she lives way too far away to make this work."

Strong winds whipped across the valley, running parallel with the runway and sending strands of his hair flicking around. Logan brushed them back.

Orion said, "Why not see what happens while she's here? If God wants to do something, then all we have to do is believe He's more powerful than our dumb mistakes. It's not like we can surprise Him."

Logan glanced at Orion, wondering what he thought he'd done.

What mistake he'd made.

"You know I'm here if you want to talk about anything," Logan said.

Orion nodded. "I know. Thanks." He held out his fist and Logan bumped it.

Across the runway, at the mess hall, Logan grabbed the door handle and held it open for the ladies.

They nodded at him as they entered.

"Logan." JoJo grinned.

Jamie stopped close to him. "How did it go with the commander?"

"I just got my side looked at by the medic and then changed clothes. I haven't talked to him yet."

"I hope you don't get in trouble because you came to find me." She winced. "I don't mean coming to Alaska. I just mean the compound."

The girls. "They told you?"

He hadn't exactly made it a secret that he was in Alaska looking for Jamie. Every time they went to town, he asked around to find out if anyone had seen her. Why did it hit him like this that they'd mentioned it to her?

Probably because he'd already decided it was a nonstarter.

Even though Orion had told him to see what God might want to do, he'd pretty much decided she was going to go back to her life. He would move on at some point.

Her expression softened, and she set her hand on his arm. "Thank you for caring enough to come up here and make sure I'm safe."

Logan didn't know what to say. "We should go eat."

He let go of the door and headed inside. So much for seeing what happened. Now that she'd said it out loud, it sounded dumb that he'd upended his life and moved to Alaska. He'd changed everything for her.

And now she thought he needed her pity.

Maybe he did.

Jamie stared over the table at the man who'd sat across from her. "Skye's husband was undercover?"

She didn't think she'd even met Skye today. Had she?

All the hotshot and smokejumper names had started to mix together in a muddle. She was trying to keep them all straight.

Neil Olsen, an older guy who'd told Jamie he was the smokejumper pilot, leaned across the table. "Finally, Rio was able to tell Skye that he was an FBI agent, undercover in the prisons for a long time. He got this guy, Darryl, to agree to testify against this bad guy, Buttles, right?"

Jamie nodded even though she had no idea. She chewed around a mouthful of surprisingly flavorful spaghetti. When Tristan had been little, he'd called everything "spicy" when he really just meant it had actual flavor rather than being bland like box mac and cheese. This spaghetti almost had a kick to it. She needed the recipe from their cook.

The warm older man who'd decided to sit with

her had a slightly gruff exterior. Neil took a bite of his own dinner and glanced at the guy beside him—someone called a "spotter"—who'd tied back his long gray hair. The two of them as a pair looked like an aging rockstar had made friends with a retired cop.

"It turned out all right in the end," Neil said. "These days Rio is the FBI field agent in Anchorage, and Skye works out of the base here. They have a house in Copper Mountain."

Jamie couldn't imagine that kind of marriage working, but then again, she hadn't been able to get a successful relationship together. What did she know?

She adjusted her seat on the cafeteria bench, the sound of conversation swirling around her.

"Then there's Tucker. Commander Newman. You met him, right?"

"Uh-huh." Jamie shoved in another bite of food.

"His wife is Stevie, a US marshal around these parts. Good folks, all of them. And trust me, I'd know. I flew prisoner transports for the Feds for years. Ran into Stevie a time or two before she settled down with Tuck."

Jamie nodded, like she had a clue what this guy was talking about.

"That guy talkin' to Tucker now? That's Mitch."

Jamie glanced over. The men sat with two women, one of whom was pregnant.

"Mitch is the hotshot boss."

"Right." Jamie nodded. "I saw them all running up the road to the base earlier."

"Gotta get that PT in." Neil nodded.

Jamie moved a meatball around in her bowl. She was stuffed, but it was so good. And she might need the calories for whatever happened next. Like carbo-loading before a marathon.

As if she'd ever run one.

"Anyway, the wife has a migraine. I should take her a plate." Neil eased up from the bench across from her, and she heard his knee pop. "We live in one of the trailers off the side of the men's cabin if you wanna come by tomorrow and say howdy. I'm sure she'd like to meet you."

"Thanks, Neil. I'd like that."

The aging rocker guy took his plate and wandered off as well. She let her gaze sweep the room. A bearded man, the huge one—Grizz— sat by himself at one end of a table. Four guys sat with Sanchez like they were her designated bodyguards. Mack, the youngest one, with dark features and long hair pulled back in a tiny ponytail, was entertaining them with a story.

There seemed to be some kind of great divide between the table where Orion and Vince sat and the other side of the aisle, where Tori talked to

Cadee. JoJo and Raine sat near each other, both reading worn paperback books. Logan fit in here, among these people who risked their lives every day to beat back the wildfires each season brought.

Seemed like it got worse every year, at least according to the news.

Jamie was glad she'd had the chance to thank Logan for caring enough to come here to try and find her. She could hardly believe he'd felt strongly enough about her to leave Montana and move to this place. Seemed like it was the edge of nowhere.

Or she would've thought so if it weren't for the warmth in this room. The camaraderie and family rivalry.

She'd never fit in anywhere the way he fit in here, sandwiched in next to Orion and down from Grizz. He had a solid family at home, one connected to this base through his brother's relationship with Tori's sister Penny, Jamie was pretty sure—she'd seen the photo on the girls' fridge. Now he had another family here with these people who obviously cared about him.

She had her mom, currently succeeding at rehab.

Her brother, wherever he was.

A job she loved.

But she didn't have a family. Not really.

Her cell phone started to ring. She saw it was Samuel and answered it. "Winters."

"Is everything really okay?"

"Worried about your bottom line again?" She tried to play it off. Right now, the melancholy feeling seemed to seep into her skin. Surrounded by friendship and yet not part of it. Uninvited. But she didn't need it, did she?

It wasn't like she was staying.

"You know I care more about you than the company. Even if you don't think you *are* the company."

Jamie wasn't going to argue that point. "Everything okay with that?"

He said, "I turned on the software and tracked your ring. You said you slipped it in your brother's pocket?"

"Which means there's a possibility it fell out." But it was the best she'd been able to do at the time.

"It's pinging live at the compound. Hasn't moved."

Either her brother was still there or just the jacket was. "Did you get the files I sent over?"

"I'm having accounting look over all the financials. We'll figure out where they transferred the money to."

"And the rest?" She'd sent over the contents of the entire network. "I'd like to know if there are any indications what their plan might be. Tristan seemed to think they were up to something or involved in something."

At face value, she'd have assumed them to be part of a drug operation or domestic terror group. But what did she know? She wasn't close to being like these people. She wasn't a federal agent or hero firefighter. Jamie was just good at math and had a knack for computers.

Talk about in over her head.

"I'll call when I have something."

"Thanks, Samuel." She hung up, aware of someone standing across the table.

"Sorry." Logan hesitated. "Didn't realize you were on the phone."

"Just talking to a colleague of mine." She set the phone face down by her bowl and finished her glass of water. "They have access to the tracker technology. Apparently, Tristan hasn't left the compound." She bit her lip.

She'd left her brother there.

Logan sat. "You're not going out there. A storm is coming in, and there are supposed to be high winds tonight. No one is leaving base camp."

"So I have to pretend he's not in trouble, even though it's possible he's being tortured for information?"

Logan glanced over. "That's a little dramatic, don't you think?"

"Maybe. They probably just shot him for betraying them."

"We have no idea who those people are. And we're not cops, so it's not like it's on us to investigate them. We both have jobs to do."

Just because she didn't like what he said, didn't mean he was wrong. The chalkboard on the wall said *HIGH WINDS*. The math beside it looked like miles per hour.

Which was when she remembered the numbers on the map in the compound.

"What?"

She must've made a sound.

Jamie got up, waving him off. She went to the wall where someone had pinned a map of Alaska just slightly above her eye level. Someone taller, who didn't need to reach the way she did with the pen she found.

Jamie wrote the numbers from memory, then marked the spots on the map that had been indicated. Not that she knew what any of it meant. Coordinates? No, not enough digits. If they had a letter at the beginning and end, they might be airplane tail numbers.

She had no ideas, only guesses.

From behind, she heard someone say, "She some kind of genius or something?"

Someone else said, "Shut up, Vince."

Logan eased up beside her. "Is this from the map at the compound?"

Jamie nodded. "I have no idea what it means though." She turned to find everyone crowded around her. Great, they were all staring now. Looking at her like she was some kind of freak show exhibition. "I should go."

She squeezed between Jade and Tori and grabbed her things.

Logan met her at the door. "I'll walk you. There are wild animals out, so it's best not to go off by yourself."

She nodded, sniffing back the burn of tears in her eyes. She could present to the board of directors of her company without getting nervous. In front of a crowd of heroes and federal bigshots, she crumbled like this was her first science fair.

Her phone chimed and she looked at the screen.

Logan held the door open. "Another work thing you need to respond to?"

"No, just a dip in our stock price."

The door never closed.

She turned to find him staring at her. Logan moved far enough to allow the door to click shut. "Jamie, what do you do for a living?"

"I told you I work in finance." And that was all there was to it.

"I know what you said." He touched her shoulder, and she turned to face him. "I'm getting the feeling that even though we were together for months, I don't know all that much about you."

Telling him wasn't going to make things better. Not after . . .

No, he didn't want to know. Even if he thought she should tell him.

Jamie set off walking. "It doesn't matter. I'm not a hero. I'm just me."

EIGHT

LOGAN TOSSED ANOTHER LOG ON the fire he had made. The one now starting to come to life in the firepit. *I'm just me.*

She'd said that like it was a bad thing.

Logan hadn't known how to respond, so they'd walked in silence across the runway, and he'd eventually figured out how to ask her to sit outside with him for a little bit. Rather than retreating to his room while she went to wherever the girls had set up for her to sleep, he just felt like they should actually talk.

Maybe for the first time.

Not that they hadn't had conversations when they were dating before. It just seemed as if those might've been more surface level rather than real connection.

Lord, help me figure out what to say.

He had been a table over at dinner, letting her have her space after they'd spent all day together, most of which had involved running from gunmen shooting at them. Of course, he'd kept one eye on her like a total stalker, half listening to Orion's story, seeing how she focused on Neil and whatever he'd been saying to her. The older man had some great stories.

Logan settled in a wooden chair close to the fire. "Neil didn't tell you something scary, did he?"

She probably had a low threshold for fear right now, given the adrenaline of the day. Seated beside him in a matching chair, close enough he could reach over and hold her hand, Jamie shook her head. "Nothing like that. Mostly he was telling me about the people you work with and all the crazy things they've been through up here over the years."

"Most of that was years ago. Before I came up here." She didn't need to worry about what had happened in Montana last year. All that had been taken care of.

She shifted her attention from the fire in front of them to him, one eyebrow raised. "Oh? I thought you said all that craziness happened with Bryce just a few weeks ago."

"That isn't what you guys were talking about though, right?" He squirmed in his seat. Kane crossed the runway, walking beside Sanchez. The last ones to head back from dinner.

Sanchez headed for them. She pulled a paper from her pocket and held it out. "When you were in that compound, did you guys see this man?"

Jamie took the photo, then handed it to Logan. "I didn't. Logan moved around more than me though."

He studied the picture of an older man with a pale-colored shirt, hands together in front of him, but the photo was cropped, so he couldn't see below the wrists. Thin. Maybe too thin. He looked like a man in poor health at best.

He looked at Sanchez. Behind her, Kane had a dark expression on his face that Logan couldn't figure out. "I didn't see him. Sorry. Who is he?"

Sanchez took the photo. "Thanks for looking."

Kane stared after her for a beat and then moved to catch up with her.

Jamie frowned. "She's not normally like that, right?"

Logan didn't know what to make of Sanchez just now either. But he wanted to get his conversation with Jamie back on track. "I wasn't trying to freak you out, leaving you alone at dinner. I was trying to help you get a reprieve from all of it—from me." For all he knew, Neil had made it sound like that stuff was commonplace around here. "Sorry."

And then she'd told him that she wasn't a hero. She was just herself.

He needed to figure out where her head was at, because he might be intent on letting her go—or pushing her away—but she was here. She wasn't okay, and he cared about her.

He probably always would.

He said, "We survived today, didn't we?"

Thanks to the Lord putting a hand of protection on them.

"But Tristan didn't get out. He's still back there."

"It's not easy to feel powerless." Logan had certainly felt that way, hearing what Bryce had gone through. But his brother had trusted in the Lord as well, and God had guided him through it. Now Bryce and Penny were healing and enjoying spending time together. Things had definitely calmed down, which was good.

Logan wanted to tell Jamie that when he felt powerless like that, he tried to give it over to the Lord. But even though she was a Christian, it seemed like there was a wall there she didn't want Logan to get past. As if Jamie had put a barrier between the strength of her faith and the people in her life.

He wondered if she might not want to hear what he had to say about trusting God.

"No, it isn't easy." She spoke quietly, as if deep in her own thoughts.

"I know you're scared for him, Jamie. But Tristan is probably glad you're safe. As a brother, I would guess he's just grateful you got out even if he didn't." Logan looked down at his clasped hands, between his knees. "I know if it was Andi who'd waded into a dangerous situation to help me out, I'd be glad when she wasn't in the line of fire."

"You don't think it's better to weather that stuff together?"

Logan needed to tread carefully. "I think he has less to worry about if he knows you're safe. He can focus on what he feels like he has to do."

"So I shouldn't have come. Pretty sure you already said that a few times."

Yeah, he had. She knew exactly where he stood. "Even if he doesn't show it, I know Tristan appreciates how much you want to be there for him. How you put everything aside and try to help him out."

"Even if it's a terrible idea?"

"It's better than feeling like you've been forgotten by people who are supposed to show up for you." He sat back in the seat, watching the fire pop and crackle, sending embers up into the air.

It felt like the Fourth of July out here—a night where you wanted to set off fireworks, but it got

dark so late in the evening that waiting to cele-
brate felt almost endless.

Sitting around outside in the daylight, waiting
for the sun to go down.

At least the fire beat back the chill in the air.

Hopefully it also helped to subdue any wildfires overnight. In the morning, they would assess
the situation, and Tucker would decide if they
needed to go out—or more likely, just where they
would be going. He didn't like the idea of leaving
Jamie and going out to fight a fire, but at least
she was safe here while she waited to hear word
of her brother.

"Your family is the best. Why does it sound
like you know what it feels like to be forgotten?"

Logan glanced over and saw she was looking
at him. "Because I do. Maybe to some people it
doesn't seem like that big of a deal, but it made
such an impression on me I've never managed to
let go of it."

Part of what he had learned about God that
he appreciated the most was the fact his Father
in heaven could stand in the gap. Especially helpful considering Logan's dad had a medical con-
dition that had changed the relationship they'd
always had before the car accident. Logan didn't
feel the lack when God would always be there.
He would never forget about Logan, even while

Logan's father was deteriorating and often asked who he was.

Not his dad's fault.

But it didn't lessen the pain any.

"What happened?" She curled her legs up on the seat, her body turned toward his.

Logan watched the jump base dog trot between two buildings and cross the runway, coming toward them. "I can't remember exactly, but I must have been about twelve, because I was in middle school. My mom worked a lot, you already know that. But back then, my dad did as well. Having two working parents meant there was a nanny who picked us up from school or whatever afterschool thing we had, athletics or music lessons.

"Bryce and I had baseball practice. The nanny was brand-new, and it was her first day. She showed up with Andi to take us home. I was in the bathroom, and she loaded up Bryce and drove home with him and Andi. Everyone at school had gone home, so there was no one in the building. And I didn't have a cell phone until I got my driver's license. So I just sat on the curb for a while."

"The nanny didn't know you and Bryce were twins?"

Logan shook his head. "Bryce and Andi tried to tell her, but she didn't believe them. She thought they were joking just to mess with her."

"What did you do?"

"It started to get dark, so I walked home. It was about six miles, and I was starving hungry. I remember seeing a stray dog, and it lunged at me. When I got home, I walked in the kitchen door, and my mom had just got home as well. She was like, 'Oh, there you are,' and no one else said anything. Mom probably thought I was just in the yard."

The next day, the nanny had been pretty surprised that there were two Crawford boys and their sister. But it wasn't like she had apologized for leaving him behind, since she would have had to admit her mistake to their mom.

"Maybe my life wasn't always as perfect as you thought it was." But then, despite the impression it left on him, it really was one small thing that had happened when he was in middle school.

Jamie reached over and laid her hand on his. "I'm sorry you got left behind."

Logan stared at their hands. "Thanks." He swallowed against the lump in his throat, trying to be brave like that night. Despite the fear. Despite what lurked beyond the edges of his awareness.

But underneath it all, he was still a scared little boy trying to be brave.

The dog wandered close enough to sniff their hands.

Jamie chuckled. "Hi, dog."

"This is Jubal." And he'd totally broken the tension in the air between them.

Animals had a way about them. Logan always felt better with an affectionate dog around. His life just didn't lend itself to him having one, never being around to take care of it.

He gave Jubal a rubdown. "I think that's why I became a firefighter. First in Last Chance County." Then as a wildland firefighter after he and Jamie had broken up, doing what he loved but as far from the pain of seeing her as possible. "Now out here."

"Because you're a hero." She smiled at the dog. "It's who you're supposed to be."

"I do it because I meet people on their worst day, and I see them with the same fear in their eyes that I probably had realizing I was all alone. And I let them know that, despite what it feels like, they aren't forgotten."

She squeezed his hand.

Logan turned his over and linked their fingers. "Even out here. Maybe especially out here because a lot of people don't have help close by. We get to make a difference in their lives and try to make sure they don't lose everything they've built."

Logan traced his thumb across the back of her hand. Not exactly what Jamie had thought they'd be talking about out here, but it was honestly reassuring to hear that the Crawfords might not be so perfect after all. Still, she couldn't imagine being twelve and forgotten about like that.

She looked at the fire. "I don't know when I first became aware that I'd have to do things for myself because my mom certainly wasn't going to."

Logan shifted in his chair but didn't say anything.

"I used to make sure Tristan got breakfast before school. I took him to his bus stop and then walked to my school." Thankfully, it hadn't been far, but while most kids had ridden bikes or scooters, she had walked on the edge of the road beside the curb so they didn't hit her when they whizzed past on the sidewalk.

"You've been taking care of him for a long time."

She nodded. "It isn't a spiral. It's just how things have always been, because we knew that if we didn't take care of each other, then no one else was going to worry about us."

They wouldn't have ended up forgotten for just one night, like Logan had been, but for years. They would have fallen through the cracks.

Who knew what Tristan would have gotten into if she hadn't repeatedly pulled him out of jams with the worst kind of friends, or jobs that were less than legitimate.

She'd stood by him when he'd faced legal charges.

Picked him up after sixty days in the county jail.

"I care about him," she said. "And just like with my mom's rehab bill, I have the resources to help them live better lives." She had left her credit card on file with the rehab center. Same way she did every time. They'd charge her for the days her mom stuck around and hopefully wouldn't continue to charge her after Mom checked herself out before the program ended.

At least this time it seemed like her mom intended to stick around for a while. Longer than ever before so far.

The dog lay down on the dirt by the fire with a groan and set his chin on his paws, all brown curly hair that fell over his eyes.

"How did you get into finance?"

As much as he kept his tone light, she heard the curiosity in his question. "I went to college close by so that Tristan and I could be roommates. We had this awful apartment on a rough side of town. I took extra classes online and worked. At some point I realized I was good at financial accounts and investment portfolios. It seemed like all my strategies paid off for the most part. No one is perfect, and things always fluctuate. It's not a guarantee of success. But I play the long game, and I managed to show my professors what I could do."

Back then, she'd been barely into her twenties and had the energy levels to pull all-nighters. To work and then study and then go back to work. Tristan had pitched in, and things had been good for months at a time usually.

These days she didn't work all night, but those early days building the business had been intense.

"Samuel was friends with one of my professors. He's my chief financial officer now, but back then, he offered me a job at his company. When I turned him down because I wanted to start my own, he offered to mentor me. When he retired, he came on my board of directors and took the job as chief operations officer."

"It's good he can keep things running in your absence. Then you won't lose income because you aren't working."

Yeah, she was going to have to explain that. And yet, at the same time, it felt as if she had to apologize for her success. The whole thing was just a giant guilt trip after a lady at church had told her she should be trying to get married and have babies rather than "seek worldly advancement."

Then again, that woman had zero clue what Jamie was accomplishing at work, and seemed to have overlooked the fact she didn't even have a boyfriend at the time.

After that, it had been easier to focus on her career rather than how lonely she was.

Jamie said, "Things are steady. A lot of it just keeps its momentum, so I don't need to worry."

"The business is solid? That's impressive, even in a good economy. Building a business is hard, I'm sure."

"Nearly ten years now. It's . . . I make a lot of money, Logan." She tugged her fingers from his, not quite sure what he was going to say.

Her last boyfriend—during the time Logan had been in Australia—had broken up with her because he hadn't liked the fact she made more money than he did. So much for being honest.

The reality was that if she had to find someone who made more money than her, Jamie needed to take a vacation in the Mediterranean and find some heir to an oil tycoon so she could marry within the same tax bracket.

"Most people get uncomfortable when they find out how successful I am. It's why I never said anything. I tried, after you. It didn't go well. What you do is impressive, and the people you work with are impressive. All I know how to do is financial stuff. I've never been good at anything else, and I try not to feel bad about my success when so many people don't have a lot of money. I know what it's like to barely make ends meet."

He glanced at her.

She could see it out the corner of her eye, but she didn't meet his gaze. What if he thought her money made him less of a man because he was supposed to be the one who provided for her? She didn't want to have to apologize for it like her ex, Steve, thought she should. As if there was something wrong with her for having the means to take care of herself.

Logan said, "So you're . . . independently wealthy or something?"

"I always wanted to be one of those people who give so much to nonprofits that they drop off the billionaires list." Her stomach flipped over.

There, she'd said it.

"*Billionaires?*"

Jamie winced. "I usually don't tell anyone. It's not as if a town like Last Chance County is going to let me live a quiet life if I build some huge mansion-castle on the top of the hill overlooking town as if I have to use my money to lord it over everyone."

"So you live in an average middle-class house and keep it a secret?"

She *had* kept it a secret.

At least he hadn't pointed out it was basically lying.

"I guess the guy who does the books at church—at all the churches around town and the hospitals and the kids' programs and the women's shelter—probably has some kind of a clue." She had the great joy of funding a lot of programs, and ones for kids were the best. Like the one she'd heard about a couple of months ago. A firefighter at Eastside firehouse wanted to start a community center for local disadvantaged kids.

She'd been planning to call Eddie when she'd heard her brother was in Alaska.

"So you give a lot of money away."

"Right up until they start calling me and asking for donations. That always seems a little off, like they start a building project and suddenly I'm getting a lot of attention paid to me?"

"Sounds like a cynical life."

"I would rather just be me, the girl who grew up in the trailer park..I like to play tennis. I like to go see movies with my brother or go to coffee with Kelsey. If the local hospital needs a new wing, then I'll have someone else write a check for me so my name is never on the side of any building."

Logan sat back in his chair and studied her. He bent his elbow and put his chin in his hand. Stared at her.

"What?"

"You pointed out that I'm a hero. Seems to

me like you help people how you can, and maybe it's no less valuable. You increase the hospital's ability to treat patients who really need it, while I stand in the gap between someone's whole life packed inside a cabin and the wildfire raging toward them."

"You know my big secret now."

"That you're a hero too? Just in your own way."

He really accepted who she was, just like that? "Why didn't we have this conversation years ago?"

He looked at the fire, his head back against the chair. "I don't know. But I'm learning to accept that God has perfect timing."

"If He's doing something, I have no idea what it is." Jamie shifted to the edge of her seat.

"That's the part where faith becomes an adventure."

She wanted to believe that, but for years her spiritual life had been . . . dry. Maybe what faith she'd had in God was a thing of the past. She certainly hadn't trusted Him to help her find Tristan.

She stood. "It's still daylight out here, but my watch says bedtime." She still wasn't used to the time difference between here and home, or the long days this far north.

"The girls made a spot for you?"

She nodded. "There's a spare bed in Sanchez's room."

He glanced over. "Thanks for sitting out here with me."

"Thank you for telling me your story," she said. "And listening to mine."

She'd had so many different reactions that she'd long since given up inviting the vitriol that came from bitter people who thought she considered herself better than them for being successful. Or people who thought her being wealthy meant she should have an open hand anytime they asked.

"I'm glad you felt you could trust me with it." And yet there was sadness in his gaze. Logan lifted his hand and touched her cheek. "Did we miss it?"

"Maybe it shouldn't be this hard to agree."

"I think we agree on plenty." He seemed closer than a moment ago, his voice soft. "Helping people who need it. Living a quiet life. That might be more than we had before."

But was it enough?

Logan leaned down until his lips were a breath from hers.

A screen door creaked. "Jubal, come 'ere! Let's eat!"

Logan turned his face away and put his forehead on her shoulder. She heard the groan leave his lips. "Grizz."

The dog shook off, his tags jingling, and headed for the men's cabin.

And the moment was over.

Maybe it was for the best. Jamie stepped back. "Like I said. Thanks."

Logan nodded. "Anytime."

And it seemed like he really meant it.

NINE

WHEELS ARE ROLLING OUT IN FIVE!"
Mitch backed out the front door of the men's
cabin and let it snap shut.

Logan downed the rest of the coffee from the
mug he'd been staring into for at least the last
ten minutes. Kind of like the way he'd stared at
the ceiling last night rather than sleeping. Going
around and around over the fact he actually *had*
been about to kiss Jamie when Grizz came out
and interrupted them. Unceremoniously calling
the dog in to dinner, knowing exactly what he
was doing.

His ex-girlfriend was a billionaire.

Did she think he'd renewed his interest in her
because of the money? Maybe it was better that
they hadn't kissed.

Maybe he should stick to his guns and let her

go back to her life. After all, having her here reminded him of everything he had loved about her.

Okay, fine. Still did love about her.

Back when they were dating, he'd wanted to protect her. The same instinct that drove him to do his job. He'd found a woman who needed him to rescue her from the things about her life that he didn't like. The ways she could wind up hurt or in danger because of her family.

Jamie was exactly the kind of woman who would confront a drug dealer and try to pay back what her mom or brother owed them. Not that he thought Tristan had ever been mixed up in drugs.

Now he knew he'd never bothered going below the surface with her. He'd only seen in her what he wanted to see: the kind of woman he'd been looking for.

One who needed him to save her.

Logan set the mug upside down in the sink and grabbed his pack, sliding his feet into his boots. Everyone filed out, and he followed the crowd toward the runway, where the plane sat with the engine running. Neil was under the wing with a clipboard in his jumpsuit, already doing preflight checks.

Jade and Cadee came down the steps of their cabin. Sanchez followed them, probably to go with the rest of the hotshots into the bus. Tucker and Mitch would brief them, while Jade preferred to do hers while they grabbed their chutes and got suited up to go.

The rest of the smokejumpers didn't much care what area they were going to parachute into. They hit the ground, they fought the fire. Didn't really matter where.

Logan looked at the women's cabin front door.

Jade said, "She's been working at the dining table for a couple of hours already. She was on a conference call when we left. Said to tell you to be safe and let her know if you see Tristan."

Logan nodded. "Thanks."

"Good thing we're headed back out to check the compound."

Skye headed toward them from the parking lot, coming from her car and carrying a paper coffee cup and brown paper takeout bag.

Vince called over to her. "Oh, looks like the walk of shame."

Skye crumpled the paper takeout bag into a ball and tossed it at Vince's face. "Want to tell my husband you're calling it that?" She rolled her eyes.

JoJo smacked Vince up the backside of his head and said something to him Logan didn't hear.

Skye caught up to Logan, walking alongside him.

Logan said, "How is Rio?"

Skye had a soft smile on her face when she said, "Fine, thank you."

She'd been gone since before dinner, heading home so she got to see her husband during the week and not just between fires—reprieves that didn't last long or come often during an intense wildfire season.

Skye said, "How about you? Jade said you were pretty cozy with Jamie by the fire."

"I'm just realizing some things about our relationship before."

Skye tipped her head to the side. "Like what?"

Logan shrugged. "Like how maybe I saw what I wanted to see. I never actually got to know her. Who she is. The kind of things she wants out of life and why she does what she does. I just passed judgment on the things I didn't like."

Skye winced. "You know Rio was undercover when I met him?"

Logan had heard the story but mostly just highlights.

"He was with a prison detail assigned to fight the fire with us. A couple of the inmates used it as an escape, and Rio got caught up in it. I thought he was a convicted criminal. Turned out he was on an operation."

"But you figured out eventually who he was."

"He protected me even though it put his job at risk," she said. "I might not have appreciated it at the time, but looking back, the fact that he pushed me into that river probably saved my life."

"I don't think Jamie is going to see it the same way." And hopefully he wouldn't have to shove her into a rushing Alaskan river the way Rio had done with Skye.

"Sometimes, being together is a little bit about being there to save each other, and it's a lot about trusting God with what you can't do. The parts that are beyond our strength to achieve a victory." She paused. "You know that verse 'for such a time as this'?"

"I don't think I'm a girl who is supposed to save a nation."

Skye snorted. "True. However, God has His perfect timing. There's a reason both of you are here now. God always has a plan, but it's up to us to choose whether or not to submit to it." She slapped him on the shoulder and set off toward the plane at a jog.

Logan double-timed it and caught up just as Jade was saying ". . . drop retardant on the compound."

JoJo said, "Do we know what caused the buildings to catch on fire?"

Logan gaped. "The compound is on fire?"

Jade shot him a scathing look—because he didn't already know the answer to that question. "As I said before you joined us, Neil and Mark went out early this morning. They reported that the compound is fully engulfed and seems to have been for some time. Probably all night. Our job is to make sure the fire doesn't spread beyond the fence."

I started that fire.

He didn't want to say it out loud, but at some point, someone was going to connect the dots between his report and this fire. Probably when he explained in his report at the end of today that he was the one who'd started the fire.

Logan squeezed his eyes shut and prayed no one had lost their life.

He left off the part about this being his fault, because he wasn't ready to admit that it probably was. He needed to get a look at the compound for himself.

Vince glanced over. "Did you see anything like hoses when you were there? Might be good to fight this residential style."

Logan shook his head.

"How big is the fire?" Orion asked. "Does it encompass the entire compound? How do we know it wasn't the wildfire that moved in?"

Logan said, "I thought you guys cut a line so the wildfire burned out yesterday."

A couple of the smokejumpers glanced at him, scathing looks. Because he hadn't been there with them.

"I'm just asking." Besides, he'd been busy running from gunmen and saving Jamie.

Was Skye correct? Had God put him precisely in the right place at the right time so he could do the Lord's will and be there for Jamie?

Jade said, "Neil reported the entire compound was ablaze. He requested the retardant straight away."

In lieu of a fire truck—which, even if there were one nearby, probably couldn't get to the compound for hours—a retardant dump from their plane was a good idea. Logan had done enough residential firefighting to fully appreciate assistance like that.

A plane that dumped foam on flames.

Or a helicopter that could drop water on a blaze.

JoJo said, "Sounds like someone purposely wanted to destroy the whole place."

Logan figured going over every inch of the charred remains of the compound meant he could thoroughly look for Tristan. If Jamie's brother was still there, Logan would find him before the end of the day.

He would be able to give her an answer.

Hopefully not the charred remains of her brother.

As much as he didn't want to be the one to tell her that her brother hadn't survived, with closure, she would at least be able to move on. Start the grieving process.

Jade lifted her wrist and looked at her watch. "Time to go."

Logan glanced back at the cabin once but didn't see Jamie.

Then he climbed onto the plane.

Jamie heard the rumble of the airplane engine pick up speed. She slid the chair back and strode from the dining room to the front door, sweeping open the cabin entrance so she could stand on the porch and watch the plane take off.

Logan's crew.

The dog, Jubal, was stretched out on the porch. He lifted his head and looked at her for a second, then decided nothing interesting was happening and put his head back down.

After the plane had flown too far away and was too small to see, she swept her gaze across the base. She'd told Logan about her wealth. The fact he hadn't immediately told her about all the things here that needed repair or replacement was a serious point in his favor.

Maybe she *was* cynical.

Jamie preferred to think of it as being smart. Jaded, but smart.

Over by the office, the hotshots filed out toward the parking lot where the school bus was parked—their ride to the front lines of firefighting. A couple of them waved to her, and she waved back.

She couldn't imagine being split across two crews with her friends, one team sent to a remote area not easily accessible, the other miles away, fighting in places they could drive and then hike to. The crews probably helped each other out if they needed it, but they'd have to know it might take hours to reach the other team if something happened. Friends who considered each other as good as family.

Jamie sighed.

Maybe she just didn't trust her brother.

Then again, she wasn't sure she trusted anyone. The nasty reality she might not trust God either didn't sit right in her heart. She knew she should. But in truth? Her actions proved otherwise.

Jamie sank into a chair on the porch.

First, she had realized her faith had grown stale. Now all she could think was how long it had been since she'd really trusted God.

She bowed her head. *I guess I need help. Big surprise. I've messed it all up again.* She sighed. *Can You help me? I need to get back what I lost. I need You.*

Someone cleared their throat. A man.

She looked up to see two of them at the bottom

of the steps. Tucker Newman, the commander, and a uniformed sheriff—or deputy. Jamie's cheeks heated. "Hi."

Today, Tucker seemed like any other guy you'd see at a truck-stop diner. Hair cut tight to the sides of his head, curly on top. An overgrowth of stubble he hadn't bothered to shave. Not the commander she'd met the day before in his office. This guy would offer you a coffee in a chipped mug and chat with you about his "rig" or his "gal at home." Yesterday he'd had on a long-sleeve shirt, but today she could see under one sleeve of his tee that he had a Celtic tattoo around his upper arm.

"Sorry to disturb you." Tucker winked, like he knew what she'd been doing and heartily approved of impromptu prayer time. "This is Deputy Mills. He's from Copper Mountain."

Jamie stood. "Nice to meet you." She shook hands with the deputy sheriff, then sat on the top step. Then she realized they might not have come here to shoot the breeze. "What can I help you with?"

Deputy Mills pulled out a little notepad and a stub that seemed to function as a pencil. He licked the tip, and she saw a flash of gray hiding in the strands of hair under the wide brim of his tanned hat. Slim hips and wide shoulders, he had to be pushing fifty at least but could probably still tackle someone the way he had on the football field in high school. Or wrestle a bear.

This *was* Alaska.

He looked at her with dark gray eyes. "Can you confirm your name for me, ma'am?"

"Jamie Winters."

"Not from around here?"

"I live in Last Chance County. It's in—"

"I've heard of it." His brows pinched together. "And what is your occupation?"

Why on earth was he asking that? Even Tucker looked confused, though he probably hid it better than her. She needed to find her board-meeting, financial-downturn, poor-quarterly-projections blank expression. *Everything will be fine if we weather this storm.*

Jamie said, "Do I need a lawyer, Deputy?"

"I'll advise you your rights if that becomes necessary, Ms. Winters," he said. "I'm aware you've been in Copper Mountain looking for your brother. Tristan Winters, correct?"

She nodded.

"Does he work with you?"

"Tristan is not currently employed by my company, no."

"Your company?"

She'd already explained it to Logan, and that was far different than some deputy she'd never met before. "Why are you asking all this?"

"The sheriff asked me to come out and bring you back into Copper Mountain. We got a report of a body washed up on the riverbank north of town." He said it like things like this happened every day. "A male, deceased. I'm afraid he matches the description of your brother, and I'm here to request you identify him."

Her head swam. If she hadn't been sitting down, Jamie would've found a chair fast.

Tucker moved from hanging back to stand on her other side, across from the sheriff. Like a counterbalance to keep her steady. It worked. A man who knew prayer when he saw it was someone she could rely on when she had nothing.

Nothing but God.

She didn't know how to ask Him to help her with this but would figure it out when her thoughts weren't in a tailspin like a plane going down.

Deputy Mills said, "Ma'am, will you accompany me to the coroner's office and assist us in identifying the deceased—if you can? It might not be your brother."

"But it's possible."

He gave her a short nod.

Jamie stood, using the porch rail to steady herself. "I'll just grab a couple of things and lock up."

She moved around the cabin in a daze, shoving random things into her backpack but remembering to grab her phone from the charger. She had another meeting soon, but she didn't have the wherewithal to figure out how long she had before it started.

I need to . . .

I should . . .

"Hey."

She spun to find Tucker filling the doorway.

"Need me to call anyone for you?"

She took a deep breath and tried to think. "It might not even be him." She pushed out a breath. "If I don't get back before the crews do, can you tell Logan where I went?"

He nodded. "Got your phone?"

She patted the side pocket of her pack. "Thanks."

"Don't worry about anything else. Just get it done, and then you'll have an answer."

As far as a pep talk went, that was pretty bad. But maybe it was what she needed to focus. Simple, logical instruction. "Okay."

Jamie walked with the deputy to his patrol car, answering his questions. Small talk. But she couldn't have recounted what she said. It was all a daze. They drove for a while, and then she was walking into a short building with a brick exterior and a glass door with gold-etched letters, empty planters beside the door.

The interior smelled like a mix of stale chemicals.

"This is the coroner, Doctor Kameroff."

The older man with tanned skin and gray hair held her hand softly. "Thank you for coming."

Jamie managed to nod.

"This way. Please take your time." He hung back from the hospital gurney, where a body lay covered with a blue sheet.

Jamie didn't look at the wide metal sink in the corner. The drain in the middle of the tile floor. The wall of metal doors that she wouldn't ever look at the same when she saw them on crime shows on TV.

She moved to one side of the bed and shifted the sheet. Doctor Kameroff took it and completed the task of pulling the cover back to reveal the face of the deceased man.

Jamie let out the breath she'd been holding and stepped back. "It's not Tristan."

Deputy Mills pulled out his phone.

"But I know who it is."

Mills's head snapped up. "You know this man?" He pointed at the body.

"I mean, we've never talked, but I've seen him before. At the compound. He was their leader."

Mills frowned. "Do you know his name?"

"Maybe Logan does? I think he spoke to the guy."

And then this man had come in right when they'd been about to leave.

He'd pulled a gun, and Tristan had shot him. Her brother might not have lost his life, but wherever he was?

He was in big trouble.

TEN

LOGAN DUG THE RAKE INTO A PILE of retardant-soaked ashy debris and dragged it back. Every sweep, he wondered if he might find Tristan's body under the remains of the compound. The whole place smelled like accelerant—not a great sign, since he'd soaked that pile of kindling and wood in gasoline and lit it up.

He turned, surveying what remained of the compound.

Even the fence was down, and every building had gone up in flames. But patches of green grass remained in a few places.

"Scorched earth, right?"

Logan glanced at Vince. "That's pretty close to what I was thinking." Along with wondering if he was the one who'd started this. "Anything over there?"

Vince said, "Looking for something?"

"You seem to have a good eye at assessing things."

"And you've got all those rescue squad lieutenant skills." Vince tipped his head to the side. "Are we swapping pats on the back or what?"

Logan had said something that had this guy on the defensive. "Who were you before you became a hotshot and a smokejumper?"

"Born and raised fighting fire."

"I know your dad was the smokejumper boss before Jade, but that's not what I'm talking about," Logan said. Vince didn't normally want to discuss his father—or what had happened late last season. The memorial for Captain Ramos hung on the wall in the hangar. "Did you ever do anything else?"

Vince had tensed. "What I've done in the past doesn't factor here."

Jade strode over. "Problem, gentlemen?"

Logan shook his head.

"Just getting to know each other. You know, 'cause we're both up here in Alaska for the season."

And they'd both been in Montana last year, so what was the guy's point? When Logan glanced at Jade, she shook her head, so Logan figured she didn't know either.

"Guess we should be BFFs by now." Vince turned and stomped off.

Jade fixed her boss-lady stare on Logan. "What did you say to him?"

He shrugged. "Maybe don't mention his father?"

Cadee and Skye wandered over then. Cadee said, "Whose father?"

"Vince's."

Cadee flinched. Her face paled.

JoJo glanced at her. "Cadee?"

"Whoa," Logan said. "You okay?" He seemed to be putting his foot in it all over today. "Is everyone feeling all right?" It was that or he was missing something huge.

"Don't worry about it." Cadee turned. "I'm gonna go check . . . something else." She strode away.

Skye frowned. "She and the captain were pretty close. She was more torn up about his death than anyone."

Jade had gone to talk to Orion and Tori, giving the rookies some pointers. Vince was at the far end of the compound, picking around in the remains of a building over there, looking like he'd found something.

Skye rubbed her nose. "This place stinks."

"Sorry. When I poured gasoline on the pile, I didn't think it would destroy the whole place."

He'd caused enough of a distraction that he and Jamie and Tristan could run, but he'd never expected it would turn into a full-scale blaze that took out everything.

"Bro, you didn't cause all this." She glanced around.

"I'm just glad we haven't found any victims."

She winced. "Me too."

Across the compound, Vince jumped up and down on something.

Logan said, "I'm gonna go see what he found."

"I'll go round up the others. Make sure they don't wander too far." She gave him a fist bump.

If not for Vince doing what he was doing right now, Logan might have figured there was a chance she'd find Vince and Cadee behind a tree, making out. The vibes between those two? If it wasn't angry tension from all the butting heads, arguing for the sake of arguing with each other, they were giving each other glances while the other wasn't looking.

Every time he saw it, Logan got an eyeful of far too much regret and a whole lot of longing.

He shook his head, tromping between buildings. Slid out his phone. No new messages or calls from Jamie—not that he'd expect any since she was working.

After the way they'd left things last night, he

didn't know what to expect at all. Would kissing her have really changed anything?

There would still be a whole lot of obstacles between them.

Who was to say it would be any different this time if they did get back together? He wasn't going to jump into a relationship without thinking it through just because he'd come up here for her.

Vince jumped again.

And fell through the ground with a crash and the crack of charred wood.

Logan picked up his pace to a run and sprinted to him. When he got to the building, he called back over his shoulder to the others, "I need some help!"

Jade and the others were already running. Jade stepped onto the far side of the burnt building. Logan put up his hand. "Don't come any closer! It could be unstable."

She halted.

"Get me a rope." He lay down on the ashy section of drywall and scooted toward the opening. "Vince!"

"Hang on! I think I found something." His voice drifted up from a floor below.

Logan slid to the hole and looked down into the dark. "Did you hurt yourself?"

"Nah, I'm good."

"Do you have an exit strategy?"

"Not really." Vince didn't seem too worried about it. This guy had been hanging out with the Trouble Boys way too much.

Logan looked at Orion, who had a flashlight in one hand and rope in the other. He waved for it, and the guy tossed the flashlight over. Logan aimed the beam down into the hole. Black. More black. What looked like a metal table. Logan saw a tan-colored tube and a couple of white buckets.

Vince said, "Thanks, that helps."

"Bro, what are you looking for?"

Jade set her hands on her hips. "I'd like to know the answer to that as well."

"Boss isn't happy," Logan called down into the hole.

"I'll be done in a second." Vince paused. "Oh, yep. There it is." An orange bucket launched out of the hole.

Logan rolled to his back and looked up at the cloudy sky.

Two more buckets flew out. Then a piece of PVC pipe and a box that formerly had two hundred coffee filters in it.

Logan blinked and watched a passenger jet make its way across the sky, leaving a jet trail behind it. "Are you done?"

"Yep."

Logan rolled back over. "I can throw down a rope."

"Great," Vince called up from the dark of the hole.

Orion had come around to Logan's side. They had no trees to tie off the rope. "We'll have to pull him up." He measured out a third of the rope and tossed the end in the hole. "Vince, tie this around your chest, right under your arms."

"Got it!"

Skye was looking at the buckets. JoJo, standing beside her, picked one up.

Orion, Jade, Cadee, and Tori got in line behind Logan. "Everyone ready?" After they'd all confirmed, he said, "Vince?"

"Ready!"

Logan said, "Pull!"

They backed up. Wood snapped. The rope slid across burnt wood, and Logan prayed it wasn't going to break before they got the big man out. Finally, Vince's dark hair appeared. He planted his elbows on the edges of the ground-level floor, breathing hard. Blood trickled down the outside of his arm between a tear in the sleeve of his shirt.

"You got hurt?" Logan didn't let go of the rope. He kept pulling. "Thought you said you were okay."

"You're the one who got shot."

"It was a graze. You're the one who cleaned it

for me." He'd been bracing with his off side this whole time, but thinking about the injury made him focus for a second on the raw skin he had covered with a bandage.

"Guess we're both fine." Vince flashed gritted teeth and pulled himself the rest of the way out of the hole.

The rope slacked, and Logan ended up sitting on the grass.

Orion clapped him on the shoulder.

Jade brushed off the seat of her Nomex pants. "This team is out of control. It's anarchy."

"Come on, boss," Logan said. "It's not that bad."

"Vince and Cadee don't get along. Orion and Tori think no one has noticed the tension they've got going on. JoJo probably found wolf tracks somewhere out here. Skye's on the phone—" Jade swung her arm out.

Skye lowered the phone from her mouth. "Rio needs to know they had a meth lab up here."

Logan's brows rose.

Jade continued like that last comment had never happened. "Vince just goes and jumps in a hole, and *you*—"

"What about me?" Logan didn't see a reason he needed to get caught up in this sweep.

"You came all the way up here for a woman,

and you're gonna let her walk away? Are you insane? Jamie's great!"

Logan just stared at her. When there seemed to be a moment of calm in the storm, he said, "You're doing a great job as jump boss, Jade. Living up to the Ransom name." When his sister got like this, it was best to just hand her chocolate and back away.

"I don't want a repeat of last year." She set her hands on her hips. "When we get back to base, we're gonna do some team-building exercises."

Vince shuddered. "And this day was going so well." He held out his hand and hauled Logan to his feet.

"Vince!" Skye called out. "Rio said he wants pictures of the meth lab!"

Jamie leaned back in the chair. "This one."

Deputy Mills got up from his seat across from her and came around to the spare desk. He'd parked her in front of a computer so she could look at mug shots of local guys, all to try and identify some of the men from the compound.

"Him?"

Jamie nodded. "They called him 'Snatch,' and I never heard anyone use another name for him. I don't know if that's a nickname or what. He's the only person I recognize from the compound."

No images of her brother. *Thank You, God.*

Neither had she found one of that other guy, Crew, in the local booking photos. Maybe it was just too small a pool of images and they needed to widen their search parameters.

She pushed the chair back, needing to stretch her legs since she'd actually found an image she recognized. How many had she looked through? A hundred?

Felt like it.

She stretched her arms, bent her elbows, and laced her fingers behind her head. Samuel had emailed twice. Jamie hadn't explained to Mills why she had to get on her phone, and he'd looked at her like he was interested in her business. Thankfully, he was too polite to pry.

The Copper Mountain Sheriff's Department had a deer head on the wall beside a huge wooden shield with their emblem. File cabinets in rows along one side butted up against a massive printer. The matronly woman who wore brown shoes and a gray skirt with a pink sweater set and pearls had a job that seemed to consist of looking over her reading glasses in Jamie's direction while manning the front counter. Sunlight streamed in the windows, between the vertical strips of the blinds.

Jamie went to the midcentury coffee pot and poured herself a cup.

"Ah, found 'im." Mills clicked the mouse and

said, "Thanks for your help, Ms. Winters. This was a big assist."

She'd explained to Deputy Mills the *why* of her coming up here and Tristan's attempt to save her. However, she'd left out the part about how her brother had shot the man they had at the coroner's office. She wasn't going to incriminate him when it was self-defense. If Tristan wanted the cops to know, then he would inform them himself.

Her phone buzzed.

She sipped the coffee and wandered over to the desk to see what was going on at the office.

Mills peered at her screen. "Says 'Logan.'"

She swiped up the phone. "I should be getting back to the smokejumper base."

"Ah." Mills sat back in his chair. "We took so long that the sheriff went out. I'm the only one here, so I can't drive you back there I'm afraid."

She dipped her head to her screen. "Guess I'll have to call a rideshare."

The matron snickered. She tugged off the glasses and dropped them to hang from a string around her neck.

"Ain't no rideshare out here. Closest you'll get is hiring a tourist chopper to fly you back there." Mills eyed the phone on his desk.

"That would certainly be faster than walking." Jamie smirked, and he blinked.

The confusion on his face cleared. "Sorry it took so long, but thanks for your help. You gonna get back okay?"

"I'll figure it out." She gathered her backpack and zipped up her sweater. It was past lunch, and her stomach rumbled. She turned back at the door. "Is there somewhere close by to get lunch?"

The matron looked up from her files. "Oh, uh, there's a pizza place down the street." She pointed to her left with a pen.

"Thank you. Have a nice day." Jamie pushed outside.

A diesel truck coughed, passing by her on the street, mud caked on the mudflaps and two big malamutes in the back.

Two older women with black hair and tanned skin talked on the sidewalk in front of the bank.

Jamie passed them, nodding when they acknowledged her. She wandered until she found Starlight Pizza and ordered a huge roast beef sandwich with fries on the side from a slender woman in white sneakers, jeans, and a black Starlight Pizza shirt.

The server had her hair tied back, but she'd spent time on her makeup and added eyelashes. The effect made her look older than . . . Jamie guessed early twenties. She didn't bat an eyelash when Jamie opened her laptop and did work while she ate.

After taking a day off from her laptop to track down Tristan, her list of tasks had piled up. She started with the quick ones and knocked out a handful, then got started on a longer report Samuel needed her to go over.

She sipped her drink, then reached for a fry. They were gone.

The drink was gone too.

Her server set down a full one and took the empty. "If you sit here much longer, I'll have to give you the dinner menu."

"Sorry for taking up a table." She glanced around, but only a couple others were occupied, and one older man sat at the counter drinking coffee.

"Not a problem." The young woman smiled. "You someone important or something?"

The nametag said *Anna*. Jamie had to give her credit; she was interested but she didn't peek at the laptop screen. "I'm good at math. I made it into my job, and now I basically have homework every day for the rest of my life."

Anna wrinkled her nose. "That doesn't sound like fun."

"Is your job fun?"

"Good point."

Jamie smiled. "Fun is what you do with the money you make at work."

"And the more you make, the more fun you

can have." Anna snorted, gently nudging Jamie's shoulder. "Right?"

"As long as it's legal and nobody gets hurt." At least, that was a start.

If she got into the weeds of how a person should live their life, she'd probably be hypocritical, considering how she barely lived what she was supposed to believe.

Why was it always easier to tell someone else what to do than to actually follow your own advice?

"Legal fun?" Anna snorted. "You aren't from around here, are you?"

She wandered off. Jamie pulled a fifty from her wallet and got a pen. She wrote *safe fun only* on the bill and tucked it under a glass. She gathered her things, and right when she lifted her phone, it rang.

Logan calling.

"Hey." She smiled, pushing open the door and stepping outside again. This time a red pickup truck passed her.

"You're in town? Tucker said the deputy came by."

"And I'm stuck in Copper Mountain with no way to get back." Not that she hadn't considered a tourist ride in a chopper. That could be cool. She hadn't seen much of Alaska since she got up here.

"We're driving through on our way back to base. We can pick you up."

She was just about to answer when he continued, "Actually, everyone wants to go to the Midnight Sun Saloon and grab dinner to go first. Their wings are *amazing*."

She said, "I'm outside the pizza place."

"Go south toward the gas station. Keep walking. We'll pick you up."

Jamie held the phone to her ear and started in that direction, raising the zipper on her sweater to beat the afternoon chill. "The roast beef sandwich at Northstar is excellent. Not sure I've got room for wings in me."

"Shame. I would've shared with you."

She smiled at the warmth of his voice in her ear. "Shame."

A white van pulled into the gas station and parked up at a pump on the opposite side from a truck packed with tools. A guy in jeans, boots, and a neon sweater paced up and down, talking on his cell phone.

"You know, this town is nice." She wouldn't call it quaint, but it had backwoods charm. "Not that I'm going to open a new branch of the company up here, but maybe I'll get a vacation cabin. Something by the river."

"I'd like that."

She bit her lip, still walking. "You're gonna stay up here after the season ends?"

"I don't know yet."

Jamie stopped at the edge and waited for the light to change.

"We're pulling into town now."

"I'm at the corner of . . ." Jamie looked around for a street sign. "Smokey Mountain Street? By the Presbyterian church."

Logan relayed that to someone else. "Couple minutes."

Finally, the crosswalk turned green. Jamie was almost across when a van screeched to a stop behind her—some idiot who hadn't seen the red light until it was too late.

She glanced over her shoulder.

The van door slid open, and three men jumped out. They rushed at her and grabbed her arms. She tried to scramble back but didn't get far. Her phone fell to the ground, and she heard it shatter.

"Logan!"

One of the men lifted her off her feet. She kicked her legs out, scratched at his arm, and tried as hard as she could to get free of his punishing grasp.

She screamed, "Logan!"

They tossed her in the van. Her hip hit the metal floor, and she bent her wrist before her elbow smashed under her. She cried out.

The door slid shut.
The driver hit the gas and set off.

ELEVEN

AS SOON AS THE DOORS TO THE
school bus opened, Logan jumped out. His foot
caught on the curb, and he stumbled but caught
himself before he went down. With every breath, he
had to force himself to drag air in and out of his lungs,
and his heart pounded in his ears.

He raced down the sidewalk to the corner
where she'd been.

Too late.

He was too late.

An older couple stood on the corner, visibly
flustered. Cars passed on the street. No one came
down the side road.

He stopped in the middle of the road and
looked around. Where was she? Logan spotted
a cell phone on the ground—Jamie's.

He went over and swiped it up. The screen had shattered, but it still worked, and it was unlocked. He didn't . . . he couldn't . . .

"Give me that." Skye took the phone from him. "First thing cops do? Turn off the PIN."

Okay. Logan didn't know why that was relevant right now. Jamie was gone, and he didn't know . . .

"Spread out." Vince headed the group making their way over from the bus. "Ask everyone what they saw."

Jade squeezed Logan's arm. "I'm gonna run down to the sheriff's office and get help."

Logan nodded.

Skye turned around, standing not too far away. Listening on her phone but not talking.

They needed to find Jamie. Now.

Or Tristan—this had to be about her brother, right? He'd incriminated her in . . . something. Or dragged her into this because she'd come up here looking for him.

Whoever was responsible, Logan was going to throttle them until he no longer heard Jamie's scream echoing in his head.

He needed to work the problem.

Find her.

The only way to do that was the tracker ring she'd told him she'd slipped into her brother's pocket. Logan had picked up the signal at the compound, the GPS having registered there when they'd checked Tucker's computer. But they hadn't found the ring or her brother, just destruction and the remnants of a meth lab.

Maybe the company she worked for—the company she *ran*—had a way to find her.

Someone like Jamie—the person behind their business, the corporation she'd started—was an asset they wouldn't want to lose.

"Skye, give me her phone." Logan motioned with his hand.

Everyone else was talking to people on the street. Asking who'd seen what. He spotted Jade a ways down the sidewalk, one of the sheriff's deputies beside her, heading this way.

Wind whipped at his hair, and he shivered. The exertion of the day and that rush of adrenaline would leave him shaky if he didn't get a handle on himself.

Skye hung up the phone. "What do you need it for?"

"We don't have time for questions." He didn't like being abrupt, but there was little time to lose. Jamie had been kidnapped.

Just thinking it made his knees weaken.

He found Samuel's number in the contacts and dialed, putting the call on speaker.

"Jamie, those were good notes." He had a friendly voice and sounded older. She'd told

Logan the guy had retired and come to work for her. A mentor. A friend.

"This is Logan Crawford. Minutes ago, Jamie was abducted. We don't know who snatched her, but they ambushed her on the street, and she dropped her phone." He paused long enough to draw in some air so his head quit swimming. "Do you have a way to find her?"

Silence.

"Samuel."

"Yes." He cleared his throat. "Logan, you said?"

"You know who I am?"

"Yes, son. I do," the older man said. "She was taken?"

"Kidnapped, yes. I think it has something to do with her brother."

Skye shifted closer to him. Jade neared them, and a uniformed deputy stood by her. The others would gather around as soon as they were done talking to bystanders. But he didn't want to stand around. He wanted to get moving.

Find her.

But right now, he had no direction to go.

Logan said, "Hopefully they don't realize who they have on their hands." He thanked God that Jamie lived quietly, not the kind of CEO whose face was on the cover of *Forbes* magazine. "Do you have a way to find her?"

"I'll get our tech people on it," Samuel said. "And I'll call you back."

The call ended.

Logan blew out a breath.

Skye squeezed his shoulder. "Rio isn't picking up."

Jade said, "Crispin doesn't get back from his, uh"—she glanced at the cop—"work trip for at least a week."

Logan nodded. "Thanks for coming." He shook hands with the deputy.

The guy said, "Mills. You're talking about Jamie Winters?"

"Any idea who might've taken her?"

Mills scratched at his jaw. "She was with me this morning. Identified one of the men from the compound for us, used mug shots. She wasn't able to ID the deceased but was able to tell us he is—or was—the leader of the group."

Skye said, "Who *did* she ID for you?"

Logan glanced at her. Mills said, "Guy goes by Snatch. His name is Ian Weiss. Born and raised outside Fairbanks but finds himself here in Copper Mountain lately."

"Any idea where to find him?" Logan asked.

Mills lifted his chin. "Because you hotshots are gonna go question him about your friend? If someone is missing, it's a police matter."

JoJo stepped up beside Logan on the other side

from Skye. She folded her arms. "We're smoke-jumpers."

"Great. So you're crazy *and* determined to do whatever it takes to find her." Mills stepped back. "I'll inform the sheriff we have a missing person. I suggest you all go back to base and let the police deal with this, given it's a crime not a fire."

He turned and strode away.

"What have we got?" Skye spoke mostly to JoJo.

Logan waved the phone. "Her company is looking into a way to find her."

Jade said, "We could find this Ian Weiss guy and see if he knows where they've taken her."

"We're assuming the militia guys have her?" JoJo asked.

Logan nodded. "This has to be about her brother. Let's hope it doesn't turn into a ransom demand."

JoJo said, "I'll find out what everyone else has," and jogged away.

All Logan could do was try to push away mental images of being delivered Jamie's finger with a request for millions. His stomach flipped over, and he tried to pray, but all he had the strength to do was breathe.

His phone rang. He had to dig it out of the front pocket of his pants. Bryce calling. Logan managed to say "Hey," but it came out pretty choked.

"What happened?" his twin asked. "Why can't I breathe?" Even Bryce sounded choked up.

Logan turned and walked away a couple of paces. He drew in a long breath and held it, wound up on the far sidewalk of the side street. He braced his palm on the side of a building and hung his head, just trying to get control.

His brother worked rescue squad in Last Chance County. He didn't need to be thrown by Logan's emotions when it could wind up costing a victim their life.

"What's going on?"

Logan squeezed his eyes shut. "Jamie . . ." He managed to choke out. "Someone took her."

"Okay. Okay." So much reassurance in his brother's tone. "I'll call everyone into the kitchen. We're at the firehouse. I'll get them all to pray. Do you want me to call Jude?"

Logan's brother-in-law was an ATF agent, but he didn't think that was why Bryce suggested it. "Just pray."

"We're on it," Bryce said. "Call me when you have an update."

"Thanks."

"As if you have to say that." Bryce hung up.

Logan nearly smiled. Of course his twin didn't think they needed to thank each other for anything, but he still wanted to say it. *Thank You, Lord*. He headed back to the group, all the smoke-jumpers now standing together.

Vince said, "White van, no plates. Witnesses described the assailants as locals but wearing ski masks. That was one description, even if it makes no sense. The rest said they didn't recognize the men, but they were lying or they didn't want to be involved in it. People around here don't wanna put themselves in the middle of a militia, so they're staying out of it."

Cadee looked at Vince.

Tori said, "What are you, a cop or something?" When Vince said nothing, she glanced around. "My sister is a private investigator. She wouldn't get up here in time though. Right?" The younger blonde woman bit her lip, and JoJo shifted closer to her.

Orion set a hand on her shoulder. For the first time since the beginning of the season, it seemed like the smokejumpers were a team rather than a disparate group of friends and rivals.

"I just spoke to Bryce," Logan said. "They're going to pray. We're going to find her."

Vince clapped him on the shoulder. "Let's go find this Weiss guy. *Snatch*. Sounds like the kind of man we can persuade to tell us where to find his friends."

"Let's go," Logan said.

The door clicked shut. Jamie gritted her teeth and tugged against the rope they'd used to tie her to the chair. If she could just . . .

Her fingers grasped for a knot or something. The cloth they'd tied over her eyes slipped down her face, and she blinked, one eye still covered. Hair everywhere.

They'd dragged her off the street and tossed her in that van.

Everything after that was a wash of rolling around the vehicle. Scrambling back when she tumbled into someone, only to bump into another person. Listening to their laughter. Nothing funny about it.

Now she looked around.

A tiny room. Yellowed glass in the window. A cabin, maybe. There was a rusty vent on the floor. Scratches where furniture had been. Signs someone had called this home.

Once.

Now there was only Jamie and this uncomfortable wooden chair they'd secured her to. She gritted her teeth and fought, but the rope was too tight. It burned her wrists while the muscles in her arms strained, her shoulders stretched too far back.

She finished her scan of the room and saw . . . boots. Legs. A person—a man.

Jamie tipped forward on the chair and managed to turn it left a little so she could see—"Tristan!" She whispered his name as loudly as she could. Would these guys hear her and come running?

"Tristan, get up!"

He moaned, shifting first before he rolled over and she saw his face.

Jamie gasped. He'd been beaten, badly. Blood coated his lips. One eye was swollen almost shut. The other blinked at her. It took him a few seconds to focus. While he did, she used her shoulder to ease the blindfold the rest of the way down her face. It dropped to hang around her neck.

He moaned her name.

"I know. I'm here, and you're here. But you need to wake up." Otherwise, what hope did they have of getting out?

She wasn't going to be leaving him behind.

Not again.

"Tristan, wake up."

He rolled to his back, his chest rising and falling fast. "What's the point?" His voice sounded thick. "They brought you here because I won't talk."

"Well, I don't know anything!" It wasn't like they could beat her for information if she had no clue who they were and what they were doing.

Apart from the tiny issue of her copying their files.

And putting money in their accounts.

It wasn't like she'd never pretended to be someone far different from who she really was. If they asked her questions, she would just channel her inner Anna, the server from the pizza joint. Pretend she was only about good times and had no clue about anything they were doing.

But how long would playing dumb last?

They might eventually get frustrated that she wouldn't tell them anything and just kill her.

"They think I have information." Tristan paused to take a breath. "They'll threaten to kill you—or worse—to get me to talk."

"Maybe we could be not here when that starts."

He pushed himself back and sat up, leaning against the wall with his legs stretched out in front of him. "Great. But there's no way to get out, and unless someone is looking for you, we aren't gonna be rescued."

Jamie hadn't even considered rescue.

Was someone looking for her?

Logan's face filled her mind, and she had to close her eyes. A lone tear slipped out at the corner of her eye anyway. He had to know what'd happened. They'd been on the phone.

As much as she'd been trying not to think

about him or that sweet conversation they'd been having seconds before . . .

She felt hands grab her again, but it was only in her mind.

Would Logan come for her?

She didn't want him to get hurt trying. But if she were honest, rescue would be amazing. Her hero, showing up like he had last time. Hitting a guy over the head and then telling her they needed to go, so determined to pull her out and save her.

Logan.

She'd fallen for him at a time when her faith in God had been waning. *Lord, I need to trust You, not the man I never stopped caring about.* The woman she wanted to be—the child of God—needed to rely fully on the Lord and not put all her faith in a man who might let her down. Logan was a human.

A hero.

He would be praying hard and working to save her. She needed to do the same. Put God first and let everything else in her life fall into alignment after that.

"Jamie." Her brother flexed and stretched out his fingers, as if testing what mobility he had. "Is someone coming to rescue you?"

"I don't know."

"They'll be back. They'll beat you until I tell them who shot the boss."

If she hadn't been tied to the chair, she would've throttled him. "Why did you get involved with them in the first place? It's not like they're good people."

"You don't understand." Tristan looked away, spitting blood onto the floor beside him.

"Exactly. That's why I asked. Because I don't know why the boy I raised, the one I cared for and nursed when he was sick, would ever have gotten in with bad guys."

Then again, there were a whole lot of things her brother had done that didn't make sense. Far as she could tell, he had no idea what the militia guys were up to. Even if he'd said he'd wanted to find out, what good was that? It wasn't like her brother had a plan.

"You don't need to worry about it. I'll get us out of this."

Jamie's heart squeezed in her chest. "Why did you join them?"

She needed to know if he'd taken on board some kind of awful mission or a toxic belief that had no place in a law-abiding society. No way would she ever have imagined the sweet boy she'd raised would turn into a man like that. Sure, he'd had some run-ins with bad types in high school. He hadn't always done the right thing. Everyone had things they'd do differently if given the chance of a do-over. No one's past was perfect.

She just couldn't reconcile him becoming *this*.

"Why did you do it?"

He stared at her. "My business is mine. I didn't need you to come up here thinking I need to be rescued." He leaned forward a little. "Look where it got you."

Jamie sniffed. Tears burned her eyes. "I can't believe I thought you were worth helping."

"Guess you were wrong."

She turned away from him, and tears rolled down her cheeks. She'd elevated herself to the role of savior in others' lives as much as she'd tried to make Logan hers. She needed to get back to basics. Jesus was her Savior. Him alone and no one else. She couldn't fulfil that role for her brother. He had to trust in God for himself. Tristan needed Him as much as she did.

And right now, alone with her broken heart, she needed Him a whole lot.

What was it she'd read this morning? The first time she'd opened her Bible app in so long.

But without faith it is impossible to please Him. "For he who comes to God must believe that He is, and that He is a rewarder of those who diligently seek Him."

"Maybe He could reward us by getting us out of here."

Jamie turned to her brother. "That would mean you believe." But still, she didn't think those were the rewards the verse was talking about.

"I'm working on it," Tristan said. "How do you 'come to God'?"

"By asking Him for help. It's a prayer."

"Sounds like one that fits right now."

Jamie pressed her lips together. "Maybe you could untie me and we could try to get out of here." Otherwise they'd achieve nothing. They would still be sitting here when those guys came back.

Tristan scooted across the floor, holding his breath . . . until he groaned. "Pretty sure they cracked a couple ribs." He grabbed the ropes.

Jamie winced. Out in the hall, or whatever was beyond the door, she heard a thump. "Someone's coming."

Tristan froze.

The door handle turned, and a man stuck his head in—the guy from the compound. The one Logan had hit over the head. Oh great. He wasn't going to be happy about that. He might even take it out on her.

The guy stepped in. "I've got a knife. Get her loose and let's get out of here. We don't have much time."

"What's going on?" She tried to look at her brother but couldn't turn around that far.

Tristan took the knife from the new guy and cut her loose. "Thanks, Crew." To her, he said, "I told you not to worry about it, remember?" He helped her up by her elbow. "Let's go."

"Why didn't you tell me we were going to be rescued by your . . . friend?"

"Because you needed to act like you had no idea, just in case someone else came in." Tristan led her to the door. "And he's not coming with us."

She'd done that before, and Tristan was beaten for it. She'd left him behind.

She looked at Crew. "You should come with us."

Tristan's friend looked out into the hallway as if she'd said nothing. "It's clear. They're outside waiting for the others, so you only have seconds. Go."

Tristan didn't give her a choice but to go with him. "Don't worry about him. Just run."

Jamie wanted to argue. She wasn't trying to be this man's savior. She just didn't want an innocent guy to suffer because she went free. Her head swam. Her wrists hurt, and her legs felt far too unsteady for her to run anywhere.

The structure was a cabin, or had been once. At the end of the hall was a door, the top half consisting of two vertical rectangular windows—frosted glass. She scrambled for the handle and stepped into a smaller room. Old boots lay on the floor, coats on hooks on the sides. Tennis shoes. An umbrella leaned against the corner by the door, a cobweb on the handle.

Tristan eased past her. "I'll go first. In case anyone is outside."

"Your friend. Crew. He's going to get in trouble when they realize we're gone, right?"

"Crew can take care of himself."

Unlike her brother? "You stayed behind. Look what happened to you."

He opened the door. A rush of cooler air swept in and brushed her hair back over her shoulders. She shivered, even though she had a sweater on. They'd taken her pack. She apparently wasn't going to get it back anytime soon, which meant the company needed to wipe her laptop and the satellite phone remotely so these guys didn't figure out how to access her confidential information.

As soon as they got to safety, she needed a phone so she could call Samuel.

"Don't worry about Crew, okay?"

Jamie gritted her back teeth. "Like I wasn't supposed to worry about you? I'm supposed to not care about anyone. Just be selfish and 'do me' or whatever that phrase is."

"Come on." He stepped out.

Jamie caught a glimpse of wide blue sky, and her running shoe landed in . . . snow? She looked around. The place was a homestead.

"How high up are we?" There were at least four inches of powder on the ground, and she was not dressed for freezing temps. Even if this snow was old enough, it'd been repeatedly packed down. Her pants wouldn't get wet.

"Shhh." Tristan grabbed her hand, and they ran along the back of the cabin toward a barn. A plane passed overhead, red-and-white coloring but not close enough she could make out anything else.

"Wait here." Tristan ducked inside, and she pressed her back to the aging wood beside the door. How long was she going to have to—

An engine revved.

Tristan drove out of the barn on an ATV. "Get on!"

She pushed out all argument or rational thought from her mind and swung her leg over, climbing on behind him. Tristan gunned it, and they jerked forward, picking up speed on the snow. He headed for the peak of a hill in front of them.

As he slowed, she looked over her shoulder.

In time to see the cabin explode.

Above it, someone jumped out of the plane. Her heart skipped a beat.

Another.

Another.

Parachutes popped open above her, high in the sky.

Heat from the cabin rushed at her like a wave. Tristan propelled them over the edge, and she saw a valley stretched out before them. Endless green rolling hills, craggy cliffs, and trees dotted the landscape below the snow line. Such an expanse that it was like being able to see all of Alaska at once from up here.

The ATV wheel caught, and they started to slide downhill.

Jamie screamed.

TWELVE

LOGAN STEERED THE TOGGLES, FIGHT-ing the wind the whole way down. Flames and heat licked up into the sky, pushing air currents toward him.

He could still hear the echo of Tucker yelling over the radio. But the boss knew that for the sake of saving an innocent, no one was going to sit back. As if they'd do what the deputy said and wait for the police to solve this.

Samuel had called back nearly fifteen minutes after they'd wrapped up on the street, having run out of people to ask what they'd seen. Or people who might know where to find Snatch. They'd been about to try a different tactic when Samuel told him Jamie's computer was still connected via the secure satellite network their company used for remote workers.

They'd traced it to the side of this mountain. A cabin.

So close he could feel what it would be like to hold her in his arms the way he used to. *Lord, show me the way.* He needed her back. For her not to have been . . . His mind could conjure up all kinds of things, horrible things that might happen to her while she was captive.

And where was Tristan?

A wind current whipped him to the side. The parachute caught the draft and sucked him toward Cadee. He steered out of the way, falling back on instinct and riding the current over the cabin, which was completely engulfed in fire now.

Logan scoured the ground for militia guys. Was this where they had gone after abandoning the compound? Their hideout had been discovered. Was this just another spot to hole up and skirt the law?

He landed on the snow and hit the ground running.

The parachute dropped behind him. Logan gathered it up as fast as he could and stuffed it back in his pack, which he clipped onto his flight suit. Each of the smokejumpers on his team did the same. "Everyone good?"

They all nodded to him.

Jade strode between them. Rookies and seasoned smokejumpers alike—and a couple of stowaway hotshots. All of them had turned up to help him come up here and save Jamie.

They'd raced back to the base camp, but Mark hadn't been available to act as spotter. JoJo hadn't been able to come, but Hammer had jumped on the plane when he heard what was happening. Saxon was the one who'd jumped in the copilot seat to replace Mark, starting up the engine before anyone could mention how no one had even known he was a licensed pilot.

Logan stared at his friends on the ground now.

Jade glanced at him. "You good?"

Logan nodded, too choked up to even tell them thank you.

She clapped him on the shoulder. "Let's find her."

Hammer came over, his pack in his arms. "I need a rifle, not a bunch of stuff." He grimaced. "Never mind. Did you see her, or anyone with a weapon we need to be worried about?"

Logan frowned. "What?"

Hammer pointed over his shoulder, down the hill. "On an ATV. One man, one woman."

Logan raced by him, all the way to the edge of the snowy hill. He stumbled on the ground, his boot sliding on a slick patch of compacted snow. The sun overhead glinted off the white under him, the glare almost blinding.

He reached the edge where the hill dropped

off and shielded his eyes with his hand. "Jamie!" He turned back. "I see them!"

The ATV had overturned. She lay on the grass below the snow line, where she'd presumably rolled away from the crashed vehicle.

Whoever the man was, he lay closer to the vehicle.

Logan dropped his gear and started to run. "Jamie!"

He raced down the hill, slipping on snow and sliding down, creating a spray of icy particles behind him. When his boots found traction on the grass, Logan jumped up and scrambled over. He skidded to a stop beside her, at least part of his attention on the man.

Hammer ran up right behind him.

Logan pointed. "Secure him!"

He reached down and touched her cheeks, patting gently. "Jamie, can you hear me?"

"This one's been beaten," Hammer called over.

Logan said, "It might be her brother."

Orion and Tori headed toward them. Logan said, "Jade and Vince are checking out the fire at the house."

Cadee came down the hill behind them. "Is Jamie okay?"

Jamie sucked in a breath and came up swinging.

"Whoa, whoa." He grasped her wrists gently. "I've got you. Everything is okay."

She blinked up at him. "Logan."

"Yeah." He smiled. "I'm here."

"You're here." She reached up and touched his cheeks, her hands falling to his arms. "Logan."

He leaned down and kissed her, intending to only offer a brief reassurance, but as soon as his lips touched hers, everything sparked back to life, like a flash of lightning starting a blaze after a long dry summer. The warmth and comfort in the midst of so much dryness . . . it came rushing in like a wildfire, and with it, a whole lot of promise for the future.

"This guy is unconscious and injured, but he will probably be okay. A lot of this beating was just for show." Hammer cleared his throat. "Guys?"

Logan pulled back from Jamie. "Huh?"

Tori snorted.

Logan said, "Who would beat a man and make it look worse than it really is?" He looked back at Jamie. "Are you okay?"

She said, "I think I'll know for sure if I can get up."

He helped her sit up. "Did they . . . hurt you?" He wanted to know about as much as he really didn't. She'd been captive for hours.

She shook her head. "I'm okay, Logan. I didn't know that was you parachuting down. We hit a patch of ice, I think."

"We should figure out how to get out of here."

Cadee came over and crouched. She lifted Jamie's wrist and looked at her watch.

Assessing her heart rate?

The younger woman said, "Any dizziness? Nausea?"

"I'm okay." Jamie hung on to Logan's arm, and he helped her stand. She leaned against him.

"I'm glad." Logan wrapped his arm around her and hugged her to his side. "I just wanna know where the men are who took you."

She frowned up at him. "They locked me in that room. I don't know where they are."

Logan was more than a little worried about the rest of the militia guys. He couldn't stop thinking about that moment when he'd realized she was being abducted. Hearing Tucker threatening over the radio to fire all of them for taking the plane out again without authorization hadn't been nearly as bad as Jamie screaming his name.

Logan wasn't ever going to forget that sound.

The others moved away to see to the male. Logan tugged Jamie around to face him. He slid one arm around her waist and touched her cheek. "I'm glad you're all right."

"Ask me again in an hour." She smiled. "Adrenaline will have worn off by then, and we probably have to walk fifty miles to the nearest road."

He said, "Saxon—he's one of our hotshots— found a ranch with a runway three or so miles west of here. Neil is putting down there so we don't have to walk far to meet them."

Jamie let out a breath. "That's good news."

He smiled, feeling the gentle pull on his lips. "Let's get you out of here." He turned and walked with her, keeping her under his arm. Holding her up whether she needed it or not. Thanking God with every step that he'd found her. "Where's your pack?" He looked around. "The connection on your computer is how Samuel found you."

Jamie said, "I have no idea. I didn't get it back. And then the cabin exploded." She winced. "I hope that guy is okay."

"What guy?"

They got to the overturned ATV, and Jamie sat on the edge, even though it was the step where the rider put their foot. Jamie said, "The one you hit over the head. He was here. He helped us escape."

"Are you serious?" He had dropped down in front of the cabin, now a blaze of fiery glory. "Where did he go?"

Hopefully the guy hadn't perished when the cabin had exploded. Logan wanted to buy the guy a burger at the Midnight Sun Saloon to say thanks for saving Jamie's life. Assuming all this made any sense at all.

"I have no idea." She glanced over her shoulder to where Jade and Vince picked their way down the snowy hill. "I really do hope he's all right."

"He's one of them." Logan folded his arms.

"So was my brother. But things aren't always what they seem."

He was worried about that as well.

But she was here, and so was he . . .

So far this rescue had gone off according to plan. Or would have if he'd *had* a plan, anyway.

"As long as you're all right." He didn't care who'd saved her. Only that she was safe. He kissed her forehead and went over to Hammer, who was kneeling and holding her brother's upper body up off the snow. Logan crouched beside them. "Tristan?"

"Yeah." The guy groaned. "We need to get out of here. They'll be close."

"Can you walk?" Hammer asked.

Tristan winced. "Sure."

Logan held his hand out and helped the guy to his feet. Tristan started to sway, but Logan and Hammer caught him. They held his elbows, keeping Jamie's brother on his feet.

Tristan said, "They'll have seen the cabin blow, and they'll come running. We don't have much time."

"Come running from where?" Logan asked, moving to Jamie. "Where are they?"

Vince shot him a look, his dark eyes shadowed, deep-set in pale skin. "How many?"

"Does it matter?" Tristan said. "If we're gonna go, let's go."

Logan looked at Jamie. "Ready to run?"

She held out her hand, and he hauled her to her feet. "I'm ready if you are."

He wanted to kiss her again, but they really did need to go.

Jade said, "This way."

She led them down the hill to the west, moving fast. Expecting them all to keep up. As a boss, she was doing great. He didn't like that she thought the team was fractured. Especially when, for the last few hours, they'd gelled in a way they never would have with team-building exercises.

A gunshot cracked across the open sky.

He heard the rumble of engines, but it was just a din in the distance. "Run!"

Hammer took the weight of Tristan and barreled down the hill. Cadee and Tori ran beside each other. Logan grabbed Jamie's hand and tugged her along.

Skye came sprinting down the hill, moving between them, going faster than he'd have thought possible on this terrain. As if it was a normal sprint and she was out exercising.

Logan glanced back and saw Orion and Vince holding up the rear. Vince had a gun out, probably a revolver he used on bears he came across in the backcountry.

But at least someone was armed.

They raced down the hill.

Another gunshot broke across the open expanse of land. They all changed direction slightly, continuing down the hill toward the ranch and a runway behind it. Going too fast to spot danger.

His heart pounded. Everyone had their stuff still strapped to them, packs and pouches bouncing around. But there was nowhere to go.

"Come on!" Jade yelled.

He must've been lagging behind, too caught up in his own thoughts.

Vince said, "I don't like this."

"You're right," Hammer called out. "Feels like we're being herded."

A rush of cold fear rolled through Logan. "Just get to the plane!"

Herded?

Jamie didn't have time to get sucked beneath the undertow of the fear she'd been feeling for hours. All she needed to do was run.

Every ache and pain in her body stretched to life and woke up, making its presence known. She'd tumbled hard from the ATV in a way that meant Tristan hadn't taken the brunt of the fall. His injuries were far worse than her minimal ones, and if she hadn't pushed off from letting him take the hit for her, he could've been in even worse shape.

They raced to the bottom of the hill.

ATVs crested the top of the hill behind them, spilling over like a great swarm of ants. Four. Two men on each.

She stumbled, her leg muscles screaming. A whimper escaped her lips. They had been lured up here to die, picked off like animals in a hunt. She was someone's prey, and because Logan cared, an entire crew of smokejumpers was going to be killed along with her.

You shouldn't have come.

Her brother's words echoed in her ears. But they were her words—to Logan. At least in her mind. She didn't want him to die because of her, but after hearing her get kidnapped, he must've pulled out all the stops to get up here.

He never would've given up.

The fact a man like him cared enough about her to come into a deadly situation after her . . . She loved that thought as much as she hated that he might die trying to save her.

Someone fired off a round.

Orion stumbled. He dragged himself up, tripping as he kept going.

So many innocent people. They should never have come for her, put their lives on the line not for a community or a family—for her.

She wasn't worth it.

Logan tugged Jamie across the grass toward where the plane idled on the runway, facing toward them. The ranch house to the left seemed empty. Some abandoned homestead up here in the middle of nowhere? She hoped so.

No one spoke. Everyone just ran for the plane, even though it would have to take off toward the guys behind them. The ones on ATVs shooting at them.

Jamie stumbled. Logan scooped her up, his arms around her waist, and they ran. Her lungs burned. Her legs. Every muscle in her body. Hammer didn't miss a stride holding up Tristan and keeping pace with everyone else.

The big man called out, "Let's go! On the plane!"

Almost as soon as he said it, movement over by the abandoned buildings caught her attention. Men spilled out of every door, holding huge rifles. They pointed the weapons at the smokejumpers.

Jamie screamed, "No!"

Tori slammed into the plane, unable to slow down. Orion caught her and helped her in. Jade jumped up behind them. The plane engine roared. Jamie climbed in ahead of Logan.

A gunshot pinged off the side of the plane.

This thing wasn't bulletproof—someone was going to get killed.

"This is a kill box!" Hammer grunted. "They lured us into a trap!"

From the front, Saxon yelled, "Get in! Everyone get in!"

Jamie scrambled across the floor. Tristan lay in the aisle. From the front seat, Neil yelled, "Everyone get to your seats! Keep your heads down! This is gonna be dicey."

When the last person got on board, Logan pulled the door shut and secured it. "We're in!"

The plane rumbled down the asphalt. Glass on the window closest to Jamie popped with the impact of a bullet. The metal embedded itself in the outer layer of the window, the plastic—or whatever it was made out of—starting to splinter. Jamie scrambled to the floor between two rows. Bullets hammered into the metal sides of the plane, and she could hear the hiss of air escaping.

The engines roared.

"Push it!" Saxon yelled. "Or we'll never get off the ground."

Neil said, "That's all she's got!"

Jamie clapped her hands over her ears. She didn't even know where Tristan was. Or Logan. Then he moved into view in the aisle.

She lowered her hands.

Saxon yelled, "The windshield took a hit!"

Jamie flinched.

"Everyone hang on!" Saxon's voice rang down

the plane, and the wheels left the ground. They soared up into the air.

Bullets hammered the underside of the plane.

It dipped a few feet, losing altitude. Jamie screamed. Logan shifted closer, fitting himself as near to her as he could in the tiny space between the seats. He reached out and touched her cheeks.

The shooting stopped—or they had too much altitude for the bullets to reach them—and she could let out a breath.

Alarms blared from the cockpit. Saxon and Neil yelled at each other, but the words washed over her. "We're gonna die," she gasped.

Logan shifted even closer, probably hurting himself in the tiny space. All his gear was still on. Sweat ran from his hair down the sides of his face.

She had no idea what kind of state she was in. Her breath caught in her throat. "Why did you come for me? This is all my fault."

"We aren't gonna die, Jamie," Logan said. "Do you wanna know how I know?"

All she could do was nod, a jerky movement.

"Because I love you, and God didn't bring us this far to leave us alone now."

Tears rolled down her cheeks. *You won't leave us, I know You won't.* She squeezed her eyes shut for a second. The plane dipped again.

Neil called out, "We're going down!"

She grasped Logan's elbows. "I love you."

Logan nodded. He leaned close enough to kiss her, just a brief hard smash of his lips against hers in the midst of this insanity. "Good, because we need to jump."

She stared at him. "What?"

Logan turned his head. "The plane is going down. We need to jump!"

THIRTEEN

SHE GRASPED HIS ARMS, NOTHING but fear on her face. He didn't like moving away from her when she was freaking out. Then again, Logan and everyone else on this plane was as well. Just because they were used to this plane and the idea of jumping didn't mean this was anything normal.

"I'm not leaving you." Logan didn't wait around for a response.

He backed out of the cramped space between seat rows and stood. Alarms sounded from the cockpit—until Saxon reached up and flipped a switch.

Orion called out from the back of the plane. "Are we okay?"

Neil yelled back, "No! He just shut the alarms off."

Logan glanced around. The smokejumpers were on the floor, wedged into small spaces. "Everyone good?"

Hammer nodded, his lips pressed tight together and nearly invisible in his beard. Tristan lay on the floor by him, his eyes closed. Hammer said, "He's breathing."

"Jade! Skye!"

They popped up between seats. Jade said, "We're good. Tori?"

She groaned. "Fine. Orion and Cadee are good too."

Vince was toward the front, a hard expression on his face. "That was a trap."

Logan didn't want to think about it. "We need to land before the plane falls out of the sky. After we survive that, we can discuss what just happened."

Vince said nothing.

Logan went to the cockpit. "How long do we have?"

Saxon had binoculars trained on the window beside him.

Neil grasped the controls, the muscles in his arms straining to hold the plane steady, his face pink-tinted. "We're leaking fuel. They must've hit the tank, because we're leaving a trail behind us. The needle's going down and so are we."

"How long?"

"A minute or two, tops. But we need enough height so you guys can jump."

Jade came up behind him. "We don't have enough chutes for everyone."

Logan said, "Can we double up?"

Saxon spoke to the window, the binoculars still up to his eyes. "We're gonna have to. Otherwise you go down with us and the plane."

Logan didn't like the sound of that.

Neil said, "There's a valley to the west. It was burning a few days ago, but the depression will give you enough height to jump."

Jade squeezed his shoulder. "Do what you can for us, but don't forget about yourself. You're not going down with the ship, Neil."

Saxon turned to them. "We've got another problem."

Logan didn't like the sound of that.

"Those guys on the ATVs? They've been following us."

Logan ducked out of the cockpit and found the nearest window. He tried to see out, but there wasn't much visibility. The engines were streaming smoke. "We're so close to the ground."

But he didn't see gunmen in hot pursuit.

Jamie's head rose between seats. "What are we gonna do?"

Those huge eyes she thought were too big for

her face were rimmed with unshed tears. "We're gonna survive."

At least, he hoped they were.

Jade came to the door and faced the rows of seats in the back of the plane. "All right, listen up. Neil and Saxon are going to find somewhere for us to jump. We can't all be on the plane when it lands. Our best chance is going to be in the air, doing what we do."

Her voice hitched.

Logan heard what she didn't say—that Neil and Saxon would be risking their lives more than the rest by staying on the plane. But they had no chutes, so they had no choice. "Chutes." He glanced around. "We don't have enough chutes for extra people."

Jade nodded.

Tori stood. "I dropped mine in the snow." Tears rolled down her face. "I'm sorry. It came unclipped when I was running."

Cadee put an arm around her shoulder. "I've got her. We can jump together."

"You need someone heavier to carry a lighter person, or you both need to be experienced. You guys are too close in size." Jade frowned. "Skye and I will go together. Hammer?"

He said, "I've got Tristan. Don't worry."

Logan said, "Jamie will have to come with me."

"Crawford!"

He looked over at Saxon, in the cockpit wrestling with the controls. "Yeah?"

Saxon patted the back of his seat for a split second. Hammer strode down the aisle, grabbed the pilot's emergency parachute—which Saxon apparently didn't think he needed—and handed it to Logan on his way back to where Tristan sat with his back to the wall of the plane.

"All right then." Jade nodded. "Tori gets my chute. Everyone else has one. We go in pairs, just like normal. Like this is any other jump."

But they all knew it wasn't anything like what they normally did.

Hammer said, "Who has a gun on them? If there are guys down there, you need a way to defend yourselves."

Vince put a knee in the seat and leaned over the back of the chair. "I have my gun."

Orion said, "Me too."

Logan didn't carry one. He also didn't carry a fire blanket, since he didn't like feeling like a potato wrapped in foil in the oven. He'd never planned to get caught in a fire, and that would stand as long as he did this job. "I have a knife. And my—" His radio. "I left my unit at the compound. That must be how they knew where to find us. They have my radio, so they were listening in."

"We were set up?" Vince said. "So we switch to a new channel?"

Hammer shook his head. "No radios. Use your cell phones. Stick with your jump partner and get back to base on your own. Everyone is on their own."

"We should meet up, like we always do." Jade folded her arms.

"That would put everyone in danger unnecessarily," Logan said. "Considering they're out here looking for me."

Everyone turned to him.

"They had Tristan. The only thing that makes sense is that they took Jamie and were waiting for us to show up so they'd have me too." It had to be that.

They thought he had the files from their computer.

Or that he'd killed their leader, Brian Howards.

This had to be about revenge, and if they didn't get Tristan, Jamie, *and* Logan, then they hadn't eliminated the threat.

"We were supposed to be in the cabin when it blew," Jamie said.

"Doesn't matter. They aren't going to find us." Logan reached for her hand, and she held on. "But we can't let anyone be in danger because of us."

"I don't like it," Jade said.

Neil called out from the front of the plane. "Thirty seconds to jump!"

Logan pushed out all thought of plans, gunmen, and how to stay alive, how to draw them away from his friends. All he had to do for the next thirty seconds was check the chute. Prep, even though they'd jumped with these already today and only hastily repacked them.

Jade took over, doing one of the steps with steady hands. "Don't be a hero."

Logan looked at her. "Get everyone to safety."

She pressed her lips together.

Vince called out, "Hey, Jade, I'll just go down by myself, all right?"

"We're both going down. We're supposed to pair off. What is your problem?" Cadee said.

Jade went over and got in their faces. Whatever she said, Cadee and Vince were being paired up and neither was arguing anymore.

Saxon called back, "Now! Go now!"

Cadee was first out the door, followed by Vince.

Tori went, and Orion came right behind her.

Hammer had tied Tristan to him, using webbing around their waists like a climbing harness. Then he called out to the front of the plane, speaking a language Logan had never heard before.

Saxon replied in the same language.

Grief washed over Hammer's face, but he got

the chute on. Clipped in. Checked Tristan, still unconscious, his head against Hammer's shoulder. He jumped out of the plane.

Logan nodded to Skye and Jade. "Go."

They jumped together.

He turned and pulled Jamie into the aisle. "Listen to me."

"I don't know how to do this."

"You don't need to. The chute will do the work. All you do is hang on." Plus a little steering. "Nothing to pull. Bend your knees when you hit the ground."

Jamie gasped.

"Do you trust me?"

She nodded.

He kissed her, not nearly as long as he wanted to. "I won't let anything happen to you."

"Logan!"

He turned to Saxon, who held out a gun. "Take this."

Logan wasn't a guy who appreciated guns, but after this, he might go take a class or something. Get more comfortable with being able to protect himself.

And the woman he loved.

"Thanks." He slipped it into his pocket, then went over and walked Jamie to the door. The ground rushed by under them closer than he'd have liked, but they could do this. "'The Lord himself goes before you and will be with you; he will never leave you or forsake you. Do not be afraid.'" She was here, with him. She loved him. "'Do not be discouraged.'"

I'm not anymore. Thank You for that, even if this goes horribly wrong. You're still God over all of it.

One final check, and Logan pushed her out of the plane.

Jamie screamed.

He gave it a couple of seconds, his stomach clenched. Her chute flapped open, caught in the wind, and she slowed.

Logan went out after her.

He grabbed the toggles and kept his focus on Jamie, watching the wind currents that swept her toward the ground. To his right, at the peak that dropped down into the valley, ATVs crested the ridge.

He clocked the others' chutes, saying a prayer for each one.

A couple of the smokejumpers were already out of sight, on the ground or over the farthest ridge. Safe and out of the way.

To his left, the plane streamed smoke all the way down the valley.

It hit the ground and flipped, bursting into flames.

If they survived this, Jamie was going to *kill him.* She screamed all the way to the ground, barely pausing to catch her breath. After a while, the energy to keep up the loud screech dissipated, and she didn't start up again after the sharp inhale.

Wind battered her, drying her eyes. Whipping her hair all over the place.

The flames from the plane were like a firepit at the end of the valley, but there was nothing inviting about it. Saxon and Neil were dead. That sweet older man. His wife was going to be devastated.

Who knew who else was no longer living?

She couldn't even think to pray. All she could do was hang on, her mind stuck between blind terror and *I have no idea what I'm doing.*

The chute swept her to some trees, and she kicked one. It scratched at her.

Jamie dropped between two Alaska spruces, and the chute tangled, jerked her around like a bad boyfriend. She stopped, swaying in mid air. Tangled in the tree.

Hanging from the tree.

I'm gonna kill you, Logan Crawford.

She didn't even know where he was! He'd just shoved her out of that plane like Rio had shoved Skye off the bridge. Sure, doing so saved her life in the end and got her away from the bad guys, but come on! This was not her world. Not her life.

A single flicker whispered to life in the back of her mind.

It could be.

Jamie couldn't imagine anything more terrifying. Alaska was beautiful, sure. Logan was here, and they loved each other. The rest of it was just scary.

A branch snapped.

Jamie gasped.

Material tore. She dropped to the ground. A cry escaped her lips, and she managed at the last second to remember to roll. Her legs crumpled under her, and she kept moving.

Her head swam as she rolled . . .

Downhill?

Jamie tried to fight against the material and rope wrapping around her. Before she could make any progress, she slammed into a tree. All the air in her lungs expelled at once, and she rolled back to stare up at the sky.

Jesus . . .

She had nothing else right now. But she knew deep in her heart that she would always have God with her, no matter what. No matter how far she went, or how bad things got, the Lord would always be by her side. Just like Logan had said before they'd jumped, *The Lord himself goes before you and will be with you.* "Do not be afraid."

There was no sound to her voice. Only her lips moved and a whisper of breath left in her. But it was enough to pray.

Jamie lay there, unable to do anything but breathe in and out, fully aware of the presence of God with her. More than at any other time in her life.

Thank You. He was with her.

A branch over to her right cracked. Like someone had stepped on it. *Logan.* He had come to find her after he'd saved her life so that she didn't go down in the plane and . . . She swallowed against the lump in her throat and tried not to think about Saxon and the grief on Hammer's face before he'd taken her brother out the door. Or the older man, Neil, and his wife who would outlive him.

Tears rolled from the corners of her eyes.

She spotted him coming and turned her head.

A whimper left her lips. *Not Logan.* It wasn't him, it was the guy from the compound. Snatch. She rolled far enough to get her hands under her, still tethered to the chute. If the wind blew hard enough, she could get dragged across the ground.

Jamie tried to push herself up, dirt between her fingers and pine needles poking the palm of her hand.

His boots appeared in front of her hands, stepping into view. He crouched.

A knife flashed in front of her face.

Jamie choked back a gasp.

"Got yourself into a mess. Should've stayed where you were in that cabin, but then you'd be dead right now." He cut her free of the chute, dragging the harness off her.

Jamie scrambled back, crawling on hands and knees. Her arm glanced off a rock, cutting the tender underside of her forearm. She gasped and held it to her front.

He stood over her. She looked around for his friends, but he seemed to be alone. He must've been on one of those ATVs. Or jumped off one and came after her while the others kept going.

"What . . ." She gasped. "What do you want?"

Dark hair fell over his eye on one side. The bottom of his jeans were wet, a couple of inches soaked above his boots. Worn dark blue jacket, thick like it was insulated. Flushed cheeks. "You killed the boss. You and your friends."

"He would've killed us." It was all she could think to say. The first thing that came out of her mouth.

"You think self-defense counts for anything out here?" His lips curled up and he chuckled. "You're gonna tell me what you did to our computers, and you're gonna die. How those happen is up to you." He tapped the knife against the side of his pants. "Fast or slow. Easy . . . or painful."

Jamie shivered, and not because she was out here in the street clothes that she'd been wearing in town—just a thick zippered sweater over her shirt. Jeans and boots.

She needed Logan and that fire he'd built in the firepit.

Snatch strode toward her. A phone on his belt buzzed. He put it to his ear. "I got her." Pause. "Okay, do that. Meet at the spot."

He hung up looking pleased with himself.

No. Just like Logan had said, God hadn't brought them this far to abandon them now.

I trust You.

No one else had the power to save them.

From the right, someone rushed at him. *Logan.* It was him—he was alive. He tackled Snatch, slamming him to the ground before they erupted into a frenzy of punches, grappling with each other. Logan's elbow caught Snatch in the stomach, and he bent forward, gasping. Logan brought his knee up fast, and the other man's head snapped back.

Snatch slumped to the ground.

Logan rushed over to Jamie. Just like on the plane, he got close and spoke sweet words. She just hung on, because this might be far from over. Logan tugged her up. She fought for balance, the world spinning around her.

Logan got his arm around her waist and started walking. "Slow and steady."

"I'm okay."

"I know." He didn't let go of her. "I've got you."

"Yes, you do."

And she meant it. Jamie was going to stick around—if he wanted, she would be here forever. No matter where he was, she planned to be right beside him.

For as long as he wanted.

No matter what.

No more rescuing people when it was God's job to do that. Jamie planned to trust Him and to follow His lead. If that brought her to someone she cared about and they needed help, that was one thing. But going off on her own as if she had all the answers was something else entirely.

Someone slammed into them. Logan went down with a cry and a grunt, pulling her with him. She hit the ground beside him, and her head glanced off a rock. Hard.

Everything went black.

FOURTEEN

LOGAN HAD HEARD THE SICKENING sound of Jamie's head hitting something hard—not the ground he was currently smashed against.

The guy on him punched Logan in the back, then on his side. Logan couldn't get up. He tried to push away from the ground with his hands under him. He flipped his attacker off to the side and rolled, turning around to face the guy.

He reached for his gun.

It wasn't there.

Logan looked for it on the ground around them. Hard-packed dirt and grass, the soil partially frozen. He lifted his knee and planted his foot so he could stand.

A gun cocked.

Logan froze like the ground in winter. Held his hands up. *Not moving. Don't shoot me.*

The man who'd tackled him pointed a pistol at Logan's face. "Don't even think about it." He spat to the side and called Logan a foul name.

Beyond him, another man had come into view. Neither was the man he'd hit with that plank at the compound, the one Jamie said had helped her and Tristan.

The third man on the ground stirred.

"Get up, Snatch. We got 'em."

He clambered to his feet. "What about Tristan? Where is that scum?"

Logan said, "Hopefully as far from here as possible by now."

Snatch chuckled. "Don't worry, we'll find him. The boys will run 'em all down, shoot 'em, and finish this."

Logan's stomach clenched. "You don't need to kill them. They have nothing to do with this."

"How about that?" Snatch grinned. "Guess you better explain it all to me and I'll know for sure."

But would that cause him to call off the hunt for the rest of the smokejumpers? Logan doubted it, but this might be the only shot he had for them to be free. Even if he and Jamie weren't.

He was even willing to ask God that Tristan be safe.

Logan needed His help to protect Jamie, or

both of them were likely to end up killed. "Explain what?"

Snatch said, "Playing dumb will get you a bullet in the leg. That was your only warning."

"You want answers, tell me what the question is!" Logan gritted his teeth, breathing hard.

Jamie hadn't moved yet.

He had no chance against these three men.

He had a feeling Hammer or Vince might've come in handy right about now, but their presence here would have meant more innocents in danger. Could he get to the gun before this guy hit him with a bullet?

It was much too far, at least four feet away.

Diving would leave him short of grasping the pistol Saxon had given him, making it worthless. At least the guy wouldn't ever know it had all been for nothing.

Grief wrapped steel bindings around his chest. Logan gasped.

Snatch came over, stomping to Logan, where he kicked him in the stomach. Payback, probably. Logan doubled over. Both hands planted on the ground. He coughed and sucked in air. *Ouch.* The guy had kicked him right on the bullet graze on his side.

What he needed right now was a way of escape.

Seemed like that was the kind of business God was about. *Help us, Lord.*

"You were at the compound," Snatch yelled at him, even though he was standing over Logan. "What did you do to the files?"

"I didn't do anything."

"So it was her?" Snatch pointed at Jamie, intent clear on his face. "Guess we'll find out when she wakes up."

One of the other guys sneered.

"None of you are going to touch her!" Logan yelled at them. His voice rang in the clearing, its backdrop of trees cutting them off from the rest of the world. Making these guys feel like no one would witness what they were doing. As if they could commit any crime, do whatever they wanted for their own ends, and no one would see it.

And yet Logan would witness it all.

His chest rose and fell, his hands still up. His knees on the ground. Three against one.

"Tell me," Snatch said. "What did you see at the compound?"

Logan's mind was still on the clearing and the trees that surrounded it. He thought back to the files. "We have no idea what your plan is, assuming you even have a plan."

He glanced at Jamie.

Still unconscious.

She'd written those numbers on the map on the wall in the mess hall. Marked locations. Even with that, he was pretty sure she had no idea what it meant. She'd seen it as a puzzle to solve. Probably because everything else going on was too much to comprehend—all the running and shooting.

Getting kidnapped.

Now this.

"Easy for you to say," Snatch said. "But is it the truth?"

"Doesn't matter." Logan needed to talk him down. "If something got out, wouldn't you know by now? Surely this place would be swarming with cops or the ATF or something." He looked around under the guise of checking for hiding federal agents.

His brother-in-law would come in pretty handy right about now.

Snatch walked behind the guy holding that gun on Logan. He swiped up his knife off the ground—a big ugly thing probably designed for hunting.

What was he going to do with it?

Logan fought against the shudder, not wanting to find out.

"Get them up. We're going to catch up with the others." Snatch watched while one guy lifted Jamie over his shoulder like she weighed no more than a sack of potatoes.

The one with the gun motioned with it. "Stand up."

Logan got to his feet, trying to think what he had in his jumpsuit or any of his pockets under it. The thing was cumbersome but kept him alive when he jumped. The helmet with its wire face shield usually protected his face from tree branches, which was why when he swiped his cheek now, his fingers came away with blood on them. His helmet was somewhere back in the snow.

He hadn't cared at the time. He'd only been thinking about getting to Jamie as fast as he could.

The guy with the gun shoved him forward. He poked Logan in the back with the gun, causing him to stumble. But he kept his feet under him, hands out to the side as he followed the guy with Jamie over his shoulder.

Would she regain consciousness soon?

She could need medical help, but they were too far from it to save her. He might wind up losing her out here because he'd walked the team into a trap.

Logan's young faith in Jesus had never been tested like this before.

But he believed God had it all in His hands.

He prayed as he walked, following the guy ahead of him down the side of this mountain as he picked his way down a deer trail. Snatch got on his phone, but Logan couldn't learn anything from the pieces of one-sided conversation.

The one behind him, holding him at gunpoint, wasn't going to answer any questions.

He needed a way to convince these guys that he knew nothing. But would that even help? They'd probably kill the two of them out here and leave them for the animals. "Where are we going?"

They had no leader.

Logan glanced back at Snatch. "Are you in charge now that Howards is dead?"

The guy behind Logan shoved him forward. "Shut up and keep walking."

As they did, Logan scanned the trees. The terrain. At one point he spotted what looked like a cave entrance in the hillside. But unless he could grab Jamie from the guy in front and run without getting shot in the back for his trouble, it was of no use.

Hiding didn't mean safety.

He had enough faith to trust the outcome, but if he did move fast, it needed to be because he felt a strong nudge from the Lord to move.

The guy carrying Jamie made a quick direction change, going around something. Not an obstacle. It was a crack in the ground, where part of the hill had separated. Logan didn't like the look of it, wanting nothing to do with a potential landslide.

It was only inches wide.

If he used it as a distraction to get the gun from the guy behind him, could he fire it at Snatch fast enough to not get stabbed? The scenario played out in his mind, and as far as he could see, his two options were to suddenly become an action hero or wind up getting himself killed.

Logan didn't feel a strong nudge from the Lord. Or the adrenaline from before had worn off and his nervous system was fried from being overloaded. Maybe he would feel nothing at all and there would be no nudges.

Just a tiny sound.

The crack of a branch to his left, several feet away in the trees.

He didn't look at it or react to it in any way. He just kept walking. Praying. Wondering.

Had help come?

Jamie had been awake for at least a minute, snippets of conversation swirling around her. She was definitely over someone's shoulder, which, given the bone poking into her stomach, hurt a lot. Just not as much as her head.

The splitting pain in her skull wasn't the worst thing though.

Lord, I don't think things have ever been this bad.

She stared but saw nothing. She listened but couldn't discern what was going on. Everything in front of her eyes was black. Because she'd hit her head? She was blind.

Someone, a man, yelled, "Hey!"

She heard a heavy thud. A gun went off. Jamie flinched, whimpering at the thought she might be shot any second with no way to defend herself against it.

The man carrying her listed to the side. She fell off his shoulder and cried out, disoriented. She hit the ground and rolled.

No.

If she hit her head again, things would be even worse.

But the momentum only rolled her away. She stopped, aware she lay on the grass. Someone was in a fight. Maybe more than one person. "Logan."

"Jamie!"

He was here. And alive—at least for now.

Jamie tried to push herself up. Get her legs under her. She could stand, but what then? How would it help her to be upright?

Someone landed in front of her.

She flinched again and shifted back.

"No, don't!" He grabbed at her hands. "Don't go too far. There's a steep hill behind you." He touched her face. "What's wrong with your eyes?"

She blinked.

"Jamie, what is it?"

She held on to his arms. "Logan, I can't see."

It was black. Total, complete black. Just . . . nothing.

He pulled her to himself, his arms encircling her. The quick motion disoriented her, causing everything to swim around her and her face to smash against his shoulder. Pain cracked across her head, and she cried out.

"I'm sorry, I'm sorry. We're gonna get you out of here. I promise you're safe." Logan held her gently. "Tell me what's wrong."

"Head," she managed to say. "Hurts."

"We'll go slow. Tristan is here, and Hammer. You don't need to worry about those guys anymore. We took care of them." Logan's strong arms helped her to her feet.

Jamie pushed back the need to vomit. She'd never been a fan of being helpless, and this was no exception. "I can't see where I'm going."

Someone came up to her.

Thick fingers touched her face. She flinched. Hammer said, "Hold still."

Nothing happened.

"Do you see anything?"

She shook her head, which caused a new wave of pain to jackhammer through her mind. Jamie blew out a breath.

Logan said, "How bad is it?"

"I'm not a doctor, bro. But sudden trauma to the head can cause temporary blindness. So why don't you use some of that praying you do to ask for that. It's pretty much the best-case scenario at this point."

Logan said, "Thanks, Hammer."

She sensed more than felt him move away, and heard him say, "I'll see what they had on them."

"Are we just leaving them here?"

Jamie gasped. "Tristan!"

He didn't sound good at all, but at least he was awake again.

"Hey, sis. Sorry I'm out of it." He squeezed her hand, but she didn't allow him to let go. "We're gonna get you out of here. Don't worry."

She bit her lip.

"Time for someone to save you for a change."

She could've collapsed right then she was so relieved. Jamie didn't want to hang on to Logan if he was injured though. He didn't need to carry her. "My legs work just fine."

Tristan said, "Good, because you'll need them to walk out of here. Unless Hammer has an ATV in his pocket."

"Sorry, don't," he called over from far away, giving her a sense of the space they were in. But with nothing but black in front of her face, it wasn't exactly helpful.

She was relying on her hearing in a way that made her feel the need to pause and thank God for what she'd always taken for granted.

Logan shifted his grip on her waist, rubbing up and down her side a little. Just enough to let her know he was with her.

She turned to him, no clue what she was looking at. "Are you okay?"

After this, she would have far more respect for people with vision restrictions. She had no idea how long this terrible blackness would last. Some people lived with it their whole lives. She wanted to do something to help them.

What it took to face the world without being able to see what was in front of her face told her exactly how much strength they possessed. Now that she had an inkling, Jamie had a new goal—a new avenue to funnel her money into.

If they got out of here.

"Don't worry about me." Logan's voice was soft. Close. "You don't need to take care of us. We're going to take care of you."

"And the fire."

"Huh?"

She said, "Can't you smell smoke on the wind?"

"That's probably from the plane, not a wildfire."

"We're not going that way," Hammer said. It sounded more like he didn't want to than they shouldn't. "We're going east because that's where the jump base is."

"What about the others?"

Logan said, "We need to get Jamie to a doctor."

She bit her lip. That didn't sound good. "Am I going to die?"

Logan shifted her around, and she felt his breath on her face. "I'm not going to let that happen."

She found his shirt with her hands, absorbing his strength for a second before she lowered her forehead and touched it gently to his shirt. If she turned her head, she would be able to hear the beat of his heart under her cheek. That would hurt way too much, and she needed to be awake, not passed out again, so she just imagined she could hear it.

That she could hear hers as well. That they beat in the same rhythm, full of love for each other and love for Jesus.

Maybe she'd hit her head harder than she thought. Jamie let out a tiny chuckle.

"Nothing about this is funny."

She didn't have time to respond to that, because her brother said, "Ready to go."

"Let's move out," Hammer ordered.

Logan walked her around something, holding on to her. As long as he led her, she wouldn't worry about where she was going. She trusted him to get her to safety.

Jamie held on to him, taking deep breaths of crisp Alaskan air—even with the scent of smoke.

The terrain changed. Her brother took over from Logan after a while.

"Look at you, the one who needs saving rather than the other way around."

She wanted to quip back that he shouldn't get used to it, but the heart to say it aloud wasn't in her. "I'm glad you're okay."

"Me too." Tristan cleared his throat. "I should probably explain. Not that I didn't want to before, it was just that we weren't safe. Anyone could've been listening."

"Explain what?"

Tristan held on to her as the terrain changed and they clambered up a hill. "I came up here for a reason, not just to get in trouble somewhere new." He sighed. "Jamie, I'm a confidential informant for the DEA. I have been for a few years."

"Why didn't you tell me?" Jamie couldn't believe he'd kept it a secret. He was doing something good, even if it was crazy dangerous.

"I knew you'd try to talk me out of it," Tristan said. "I'm not good at much. I don't have that many options. Things haven't been perfect, but it's a decent gig."

"And you'll be able to take what we downloaded and turn it over to the DEA?"

"Maybe some good will come out of this mess after all." He slowed them to a stop.

The air smelled cleaner, and it was cooler. Had

they reached the summit? Jamie couldn't see it, though she did feel as if the dark wasn't quite so black. Probably just her imagination wishing for things to be different. But then, her brother was safe, and Logan was here.

Maybe things didn't need to be different.

She heard the rumble of a small engine and flinched.

"It's just Logan and Hammer. They found a couple of the ATVs, must've belonged to Snatch and his friends."

The engines neared.

Tristan led her to one, and she climbed on. Logan tugged her arms around his waist and said, "You good?"

She clung to his strength. "I love you."

Logan twisted around in her arms, touched her cheek and kissed her. It felt different than it ever had before, maybe because her vision was being denied her and everything else seemed so much more vibrant. She could focus on the touch of his lips on hers so much more than any other time.

"Don't let go." His voice was husky, and she could hear the worry in his tone.

Jamie wasn't going to do that.

Not ever.

FIFTEEN

WE'VE GOT IT FROM HERE."

Logan said "She can't see" for like the fifth time since they'd pulled into the hospital under sheriff's office escort and he'd carried Jamie through the emergency room doors.

The nurse nodded. She and two others, one of whom was a doctor, wheeled Jamie away down the hall. Tristan had insisted on walking under his own steam, though Hammer went with him.

Deputy Mills clapped him on the shoulder. "I gotta go call Sheriff Starr. I'll be back, so don't go anywhere."

Logan nodded absently. Jamie was going to be fine, right? He half expected Bryce to call and ask if everything was all right. Logan figured he'd head it off and sent his brother a text that they were at the hospital and to keep praying that Jamie would be all right.

Hammer strode around the corner at the end of the hall.

When he was close enough, Logan held his hand out.

Hammer grabbed it, then pulled him in and clapped him on the back.

"Thank you for being there." Logan cleared his throat.

His fellow firefighter had probably saved all their lives by helping him take down the three men. Tristan had been a great distraction. Logan had jumped on one. That Hammer had taken out the other two and no one was shot in the process was pretty amazing.

"I'm glad I was." Hammer squeezed Logan's hand, then let go. "Any news on the others?"

Logan shook his head.

Hammer's attention snagged on something over Logan's shoulder. "Looks like we might find out something."

The doors swished open. Skye and a big guy in a suit came in, Jade between them. The smoke-jumper boss hopped with one foot in the air. She spotted them, and her expression immediately changed, pain switching to relief. "Is anyone else here?"

Logan and Hammer met them halfway. "You're the first we've seen. What happened?"

Skye said, "She turned her ankle when we hit the ground."

A guy in red scrubs came over with a wheelchair, and Jade sat. He wheeled her away, and she leaned over the arm of the chair to call back to them, "No one leaves without checking in with me first."

He was glad they were all right. But what about the rest of their team? Leaving them hadn't felt good, even though he'd had no idea how to round up a group that had scattered in all directions.

"Guys," Skye said. "Rio is here."

The FBI agent.

"Babe, you remember Logan and Hammer."

"Good to see you guys again." Rio shook their hands. "I saw Deputy Mills outside. That's how you got here?"

Logan said, "We figured we could use some help, so as soon as we were within cell range, we called for a ride."

Rio grinned. "I bet he loved that."

"He did mumble something about Uber when he showed up." Logan didn't understand it, but Jamie evidently thought it was funny. "You and Jade found Rio?"

Skye said, "We did the same as you, only I called the Feds, not the sheriff." She winked and

Hammer chuckled. "Jade spent the whole ride over on the phone with Tucker. He's got the retardant plane in the air, and Mark went up as their spotter. The two helos are out as well. If our people are in the open, they should be able to find them."

"I hope so." Hammer was about to continue, but his phone rang. "Sorry." He dug it out of his pocket, and Logan got a look at how grimy he was.

Pretty much the same as Logan, covered in sweat and dirt.

Hammer frowned at the screen. He put it to his ear. "Sax?"

Logan's brows rose.

"Yeah. You're good?" Relief washed over Hammer's face. "That's good news. Yeah, I'll tell them. Call Tucker for a pickup. Keep your heads down." He hung up and said, "Saxon got himself and Neil out. Neil is in bad shape, but he's alive. Saxon will get him here."

Skye leaned against her husband's arm, clasping his hand.

"That's good news," Logan said. He squeezed Hammer's shoulder. The guy looked a little shell-shocked. "Great news."

Hammer nodded. "I need to call Mack."

Logan trudged to the nearest chair and sat. All his energy soaked into the floor under his feet.

He ran his hands down his face. "It feels like it should be over because we're here, but half the team is still out there."

Skye sat across from him. "Rio was already heading to my last location. That's how he found us so fast."

Her husband settled beside her. "I got intel this morning from a contact of mine that the militia had put out a hit on all the smokejumpers. When I couldn't contact Skye, I headed for her location." He reached over and took her hand. Partners. A couple who showed up for each other the way Jamie did for her family. The way Logan had for her.

The way he wanted to keep doing.

But with the team out there, he couldn't relax. He had to keep praying. "The helos and the plane will find them, right?"

Skye nodded. "That's what I'm asking God for."

He looked at Rio. "Your contact . . . was it Tristan Winters?"

Rio looked confused.

"He said he's an informant for the DEA. That's why he was up here with the militia."

"Any idea what they're up to?" The way Rio said it made it sound like a loaded question.

"We have copies of their files, but even Tristan didn't know."

Rio scratched his jaw. "Can I get copies of that stuff?"

Logan said, "Soon as Jamie lets me know what happened to the laptop." He wasn't sure she wanted Rio to know she had given the militia money, even if it was just to see what they did with it.

He should call Samuel.

And his family in Last Chance County.

Her mom too, maybe. If he could find the number for the place where she was in treatment.

"I appreciate it," Rio said. "I've been looking at these people for a long while, and none of it makes sense. We need a break in this case. And by 'we,' I mean me." He pointed at himself, giving them both a look.

Logan lifted his hands. "I already have a job. I don't want to help with yours."

"Good. I'm glad we're clear about that."

Skye's lips curled up at the corners. "I'll reiterate that with the others the first chance I get—when everyone is back at the jump base and we can have a boring briefing like it's any other day and nothing crazy happens."

"I'm going back to the office." Rio kissed the back of Skye's hand, still clasped in his. "If I can get your friends' cell providers to give us access to their phones, we can run the GPS. Skye, you get to a computer and look up their tracker rings.

Try and find them that way if the plane and the helos have no luck."

He wandered out, and Deputy Mills came back in. "Logan?"

He nodded.

"The man with you and Ms. Winters . . . can you tell me who that was?"

"The one with the beard or the injured guy?" He had no idea if Mills was asking about Hammer or Tristan.

"I guess I'll go find out." Mills headed down the hall, away from them.

Skye said, "I wonder what that was about."

Logan had no idea and no energy to do more than shake his head. Maybe the sheriff's office had a reason to talk to Tristan. Something Logan knew about—or something he didn't. Who knew? There would be a whole lot of paperwork after today. Probably a few reprimands from Tucker, though that guy of all people knew you put it all on the line for the woman you loved. He'd faced his share of gunmen protecting his.

Skye said, "You did good today."

He frowned at her. "What do you mean?"

"Kept it tight," she said. "You'll make a great jump boss. Probably sooner rather than later."

"You think I had it together? I led us into a trap and nearly got us all killed. Someone might be dead because of me."

"You were solid. You held on." She nodded. "That's all it takes."

Maybe what she'd seen on the exterior had painted a different picture than what had been going on in his heart and mind.

"When she wakes up, you can ask her to marry you." Skye grinned as if she felt the need to laugh at her own joke. "You'll wanna keep that woman around."

"That, you *didn't* need to tell me. I already knew."

"Smart man." Skye stood. "I'll be back with coffee, and hopefully there will be news about the others."

Jamie blinked, her vision blurry, but the fact she could see anything right now was a blessing. "Logan?"

The man eased against the side of her hospital bed. "Sorry, just me."

"Tristan." Jamie held out her hand. "You're okay?"

"No, but I will be." He squeezed her fingers. "I got checked out. Kind of. There was a cop asking for me, so I ditched and came in here."

"You're leaving?" She heard the intent in his tone.

"Not without saying goodbye this time."

The tightness in her chest eased. Her head still seriously pounded, but she could at least manage the pain with the help of the meds a nice doctor with a gentle voice had given her. If he came back in, she wouldn't even recognize him, given she hadn't seen his face. He had told her that she would get her vision back soon enough but to be patient and let her body heal.

Tristan cleared his throat. "Thanks for coming to find me, to make sure I was all right."

"But..."

He chuckled. "But you're off duty as of now. And that lasts forever. If Logan gets in trouble, feel free to go after him. But I'm good, okay?"

Jamie didn't like the sound of that, but she would be trusting God every day for her brother's protection.

"You don't agree."

Jamie said, "Maybe if at some point you need something that requires my particular skills..."

"Being annoying and relentless?"

She smiled. "That isn't what I was talking about."

He squeezed her hand. "Yeah, sis. I'll call you."

"Thank you."

"I appreciate it," he said. "Everything, I mean. I know what you did for me. I know what you sacrificed."

She didn't need him to finish. Not when

tears were already rolling down her cheeks. This sounded way too much like goodbye. "You are going to come back. Or I will hunt you down."

Tristan said, "Fine. I'll call or send a text or something."

She figured he could do better than that if he wanted her to know he was all right. Still, she said, "I'd appreciate it. I worry about you."

"Like I said, you're off duty."

She smiled. In her mind, she saw him at eight years old, stomping his foot and demanding another cookie when she'd told him he could only have one.

"Are you gonna be okay?"

"I think so." She bit her lip. Everything was changing. She could tell.

It wasn't all bad, but she had never dealt well with shifts. Samuel could attest to that. But when the evidence was clear that things needed to change, she could accept that it was for the better. Like Tristan. She wanted to pray that he would find something "better." Even if he was doing something good, she wanted more for him.

"Let Logan take care of you."

Jamie nodded, swiping at the tears. Her brother handed her a tissue. He really was leaving. "Where are you going to go?"

"I can't get ahold of my DEA contact, the special agent who is my handler or whatever they call it. I should probably find out if he's okay, see if something happened."

"I hope he's all right." Earlier today, she hadn't even known her brother had anything to do with a federal agent. If she had, she'd have assumed he was being investigated by one.

Now it was like she'd never met this man sitting with her.

The boy she'd raised.

Take care of him, Lord.

Tristan said, "Me too." Then leaned down and kissed her forehead. "See you soon, sis." He stopped at the door. "Logan is here."

She glanced at the door and only saw a dark figure. She followed him around the end of the bed, tracking him with her gaze, and he sat beside her hip. Dark clothes. He smelled faintly of smoke and sweat, the quintessential Logan scent under it all.

"You can see me."

She smiled. "I like the sound of your voice."

He said, "You get your sight back and that's what you say?"

Her cheeks heated. Maybe they shouldn't have this conversation now. "I can't *see* you. Just a shape, like I have super bad eyesight."

He leaned in, close enough that his nose almost touched hers. "How about now?"

She tried not to laugh. "I don't think it works like that."

She'd been so scared before. Now she was finding the humor, because of Logan.

He shifted on the side of the bed as if he really was settling in for the long haul. "I'll stick around. The doctor can fill me in."

"What about the other smokejumpers? Is everyone okay?"

Logan said, "Jade and Skye, Hammer, me and you, and Tristan have made it back so far. Saxon and Neil survived, which was probably a total miracle. I'm sure Saxon will have to tell the story several times around the fire."

"And the others?"

"Orion and Tori and Vince and Cadee are missing still." He held her hand. "But we have people out looking for them."

"We should pray."

"You care about them."

"Of course," Jamie said. "They're the best kind of people."

"They go all out to have each others' backs. Just like you," Logan said. "They aren't perfect. In fact, some of them don't get along well at all. But I know they'll be okay out there. They have God watching out for them, and they have each other."

Jamie told him what Tristan had said about going to find out if his handler was all right. "I

LISA PHILLIPS

have no idea if he'll be okay or even much of what this was all about."

"I know. We still have no idea what those people were up to. But their leader is dead, and Snatch took over to fill the void. Now he's dead, thanks to Hammer's quick reflexes."

"He's dead?"

Logan said, "Yes. You don't have to worry about him."

A shudder that was a whole lot of relief rolled through her.

"Whoever takes over won't have any idea who you are." Logan rubbed his thumb across the back of her hand. "You won't be in danger, but . . . do you want to stick around the base for a while?"

"I hadn't even thought about how long I'll be here."

"You probably want to get back to Last Chance County."

She shook her head. "I meant in the hospital. The doctor said I should stay at least overnight, just under observation. Since I hit my head and blacked out."

"Ah, I see."

"After that, I think the girls will let me stay. I'd like to be here to find out when the others are located. And I want to spend time with you."

Logan let out a breath—an audible exhale.

"I'm glad to hear it." He laughed for a second, and it sounded almost nervous. "I wasn't sure."

"If you aren't going anywhere, then neither am I. Besides, the girls invited me to the Bible study they do on Sundays, and I want to be here for it." She could work from anywhere.

Thinking about it in terms of her being mobile with her job didn't sound super romantic, but she and Logan fitted together the way her job fitted who she was. It was as simple and as profound as that.

She'd loved him forever.

Her heart had never let go of the fire that had burned for him.

Rather than overcoming the obstacles between them, she was a different person now in a way that seemed to have resolved their issues. "I once was blind, but now I see."

"Fits, doesn't it?" he said. "I was thinking about the same hymn the day I found you. *How sweet the sound.*"

"It is sweet, isn't it?"

"All of it. You, me. The grace of God. I wouldn't have said I was the kind of guy who was looking for sweet like that, but I certainly found it."

"Or it found you."

Logan leaned down slowly. She touched his face, able to make out the line of his jaw. She traced the warmth of his skin. Then he touched his lips to hers, and the fire in her flared to life again, the same way it did whenever he was near.

Being here with him, sharing this moment, felt familiar in a comforting way and new at the same time. As if she was rediscovering something. And opening a gift she'd never been given before.

Jamie let it sweep over her, the first of many moments between them.

Ones that felt like they could last a lifetime.

Because God, in His grace, had chosen to take a wretch like her and lift her up. He'd invited her into His family and given her more than she'd ever believed she deserved.

And when she'd thought she had everything? He'd given her this wonderful man as well.

Thank You.

THANK YOU

Thank you so much for reading *Burning Hearts*. We hope you enjoyed the story. If you did, would you be willing to do us a favor and leave a review? It doesn't have to be long- just a few words to help other readers know what they're getting. (But no spoilers! We don't want to wreck the fun!) Thank you again for reading!

We'd love to hear from you—not only about this story, but about any characters or stories you'd like to read in the future. Contact us at www.sunrisepublishing.com/contact.

READ ON FOR MORE FROM

CHASING FIRE:
ALASKA

Gear up for the next Chasing Fire: Alaska romantic suspense thriller, Burning Rivals by Lisa Phillips and Voni Harris.

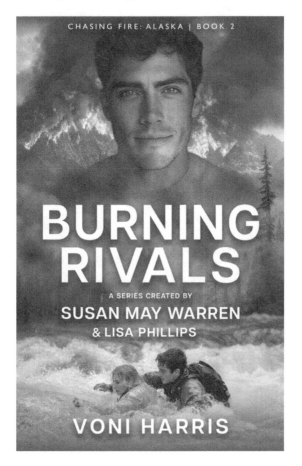

CHASING FIRE: ALASKA | BOOK 2

BURNING RIVALS

A SERIES CREATED BY

SUSAN MAY WARREN
& LISA PHILLIPS

VONI HARRIS

RESCUE. DANGER. DEVOTION.
THIS TIME, THEIR HEARTS ARE ON
THE LINE.

He lost the one person who meant the most to him—and she let it happen.

Vince hasn't forgiven Cadee for abandoning his father in the fire that took his life, but he's going to find out why. When he discovers the Feds have a warrant out for his arrest, he knows he's being framed for crimes he didn't commit. And Cadee might be the only one he can rely on to clear his name. Vince will have to confront his bitter past and put his unwavering trust in the woman who once shattered his heart.

And Cadee...well, she knows better than to open up her heart—and trust—to the man who hates her. But she needs him if she hopes to stay alive, so...

Oh, it's going to be a long, hot summer.

Grab this sizzling but clean romantic adventure through the fiery forest of Alaska in this latest installment of the Chasing Fire: Alaska series.

Keep reading for a sneak peek...

ONE

CADEE MOORE HAD NEVER RUN FROM a fight, and running today might well cost her life.

"Thirty seconds to jump!" Neil, their pilot, called back from the cockpit of the Midnight Sun smokejumping plane.

In all her years of being a hotshot, and now a smokejumper, Cadee Moore had never run from gunmen on ATVs to a plane, been shot at as the plane took off...or known for certain their plane was going to crash.

She gripped the armrests.

In the front row next to Vince Ramos, she could see past him out the window to where smoke billowed from each engine. The plane shook hard, bucked side to side. Her stomach swished around with it.

God!

She reached down and pulled out her parachute and her fire pack from under her seat.

Jumping from a plane streaming smoke was not a thing she'd ever expected as a smokejumper. She twisted the tracker ring Jade had given all the Midnight Sun SJs.

They'd barely made it off the ground before guns had begun shooting at the plane.

They had parachutes, and they had a pilot still doing his best to get them as high as possible and as far as possible from the militiamen.

But the crash was going to happen.

Vince adjusted the straps of his fire pack on his lap and shot her the hard glance she'd lately grown accustomed to, frowning, his dark eyebrows meeting in the middle. Because he thought she was scared?

He called out, "Hey, Jade, I'll just go down by myself, all right?"

"We're both going down. We're supposed to pair off. What is your problem?" Okay, she sounded just as antagonistic as he had.

Jade leaned into their space, her brown eyes blazing. Her voice was scarily steady and quiet.

"The two of you and your constant bickering is why I assigned you as partners." She sighed. "You jump first. Together." She stood straight. "You're grownups. Work. It. Out. Have each other's backs." Her dark-blonde braid swung as she turned to help Logan adjust his chute.

Cadee and Vince looked at each other. He dipped his head to her, and she returned it. She would have his back. It seemed like he'd have hers. She focused her attention on her own chute.

What is his problem anyway?

No matter how hard he pushed, she couldn't back down until she knew *why* he treated her like this.

The rest of the Midnight Sun crew was, well...neutral toward her.

Vince...not so much. He was never anything but angry at her. Never did anything but dig into her.

At one time, she and Vince had dated. They'd been in love, and she'd thought it would last forever. Until he'd broken it off. For no reason she understood.

These days she didn't understand Vince at all.

The plane tilted nose first, and they screamed toward the earth…for a second or two. But Neil was a top-notch pilot.

She quickly patted over her fire pack, even though she'd already triple-checked it.

"Now! Go now!" Saxon, the spotter, called over his shoulder from the cockpit.

Cadee jumped up, stepped into her fire pack, and popped into the aisle. She adjusted her bright orange Nomex fire jacket and put on her helmet. Well, she called it a head cage.

Behind her, Vince tugged at her parachute.

She turned and tugged at his straps. They fist-bumped. Trusting Vince was not the issue. This was the man she'd dated while they were in the Ember training program together. The man for whom her feelings were still alive. Even if she would never admit it.

Jade opened the hatch, and Cadee stood in the opening.

Thump, thump. Jade tapped her shoulders, and Cadee jumped out of the plane.

The noise of the wind filled her ears as she fell through the air. The chute opened, popped her up. Now she was floating, not falling, and there was peaceful quiet.

Or at least, there soon would be.

She teared up at the whine of the plane falling. Other smokejumpers fell out, and she prayed their chutes caught them. The red-and-white aircraft dipped toward the ground in front of her. It streamed with smoke, flipped, then hit the ground.

Flames exploded into the air.

Fighting the toggles, she twisted her head and counted parachutes. The wind seemed to be separating them all over the place, but she spotted everyone. *Thank God.* "God, protect the SJs. Please. Please." The mossy forest below was a beautiful soft green dotted by fireweed and other wildflowers, but she couldn't enjoy the view. She was squinting, looking for ATVs.

Vince was close, floating down with her.

Since Vince had been brought onto Midnight Sun this season, they hadn't even had short conversations. Just fights. She was so tired of it. When Jade had made them partners, it'd gotten even worse. She didn't even know

Vince anymore. Worse, when he was around, she didn't know *herself* anymore either.

But they were supposed to work together. Jade was right. Bickering would get them both killed—and maybe everyone else on the team as well.

She wrestled the toggles. Cadee looked down at the spruce trees reaching up to them, swaying. This was a crazy wind.

And who knew what was going to happen? The militia wanted them all dead. Those guys with guns were probably down there waiting for them.

God!

She scanned the ridgeline. The valley floor. And a jolt of recognition shook through her.

Cadee knew about where she and Vince were. She'd grown up around here.

Ingriq Village was at least fifteen miles to the southeast. She could already see the ribbon of the river where she and her sister, Emma, had spent countless hours. The paved road from the village to Copper Mountain cut through the beauty of the land.

And at the end of that road...safety.

If they could outrun the guys with the guns.

The last thing Vince Ramos wanted was his life in Cadee Moore's hands.

He held his steering lines tight, but the air shifted so hard they were nearly useless.

If he'd believed God was in control, he might've thanked Him for the parachute. But the wind might still kill him. Was God going to take care of that? He hadn't taken care of the Midnight Sun crew's plane. Or the adrenaline of surviving the crash.

It was parachutes that had taken care of the team—he hoped.

They'd at least taken care of himself and Cadee.

So far.

But it was the parachutes, not God.

And he and Cadee would have to somehow deal with the partnership Jade had forced them into, as well as with their conflict. And they'd have to do it *themselves*.

Vince looked over at her. Her creamy skin had turned ruddy, and her dark-brown ponytail

with blonde highlights was chaos. She was bat-
tling the wind too, and handling it well. But as
soon as they reached the ground, there would
be no more peaceful quiet.

The training at the extra-tough Ember, Montana, smokejumping program had been a test of
his skills. Cadee's too. They had both pursued
that training because they knew Alaska would
be a tough place to serve, and they'd both been
gunning for the Midnight Sun SJ crew. But
Ember was where the training program was run
by those legendary smokejumpers that people
wrote books about. Jed Ransom. Tucker Newman—now their commander.

Still, his only goal had been coming to
Alaska.

Vince had been in college when Dad had
become the Midnight Sun smokejumper boss,
and he'd wanted to learn from that man. And
get away from his DEA job.

Cadee had grown up in Alaska, and her heart
was here. They'd both finished the training
course, but she'd completed it slightly ahead of
him—and Midnight Sun had only had one slot.

The bosses had given it to Cadee, and she'd

gone home. He'd stayed in Montana and worked last year's fire season as a smokejumper in Ember while she'd been in Alaska, working under his father.

Nine months ago, his dad had died at the Aktuvik fire.

He stopped that thought process to focus on steering through the harsh wind.

He finally saw a very small meadow surrounded by Sitka spruce up ahead. The wind was thankfully sending them that direction. He pointed at it, shouted over to Cadee.

When the ground finally showed up, he rolled to his knees. He stood up, gathered his chute fast, and ran to the edge of the meadow to make room for her to land.

Wait.

Where was Cadee?

He turned a three sixty, seeing only moss, grass, trees. "Cadee!" he shouted.

"Stupid wind blew me into this spruce, Vince," she called.

He looked up, shrugged out of his parachute straps, and ran over as fast as he could.

"You didn't land a perfect jump, did you?"

He shook his head to clear his stupidity. He hadn't meant for it to come out that way. He didn't know why every word that issued from his mouth around her was antagonistic. Why did he always act like this near her?

Right.

He knew why. This was the woman who had cost him his father.

He stood under the tree and looked up to see the mess the wind had made for her. He saw how to get her down. "Just a minute. I've got you."

"Are you serious?" Cadee twisted around gently, looking up and examining how the parachute cord had trapped her in the tree. "I'm fine. I can take care of myself, thank you very much."

He opened his mouth to respond. Closed it. He'd probably deserved that, the way he'd been laying into her lately.

She reached up and took hold of the thick limb she was hanging from with both hands, swung her legs once, twice. The third time, her legs grabbed the limb, and she pulled herself up.

Okay, he had some abs, but this reminded

him to level up his core exercises. A couple levels.

"Great job. I'll help..."

She glared down at him and stood on the limb.

Fine. He closed his mouth again and just stood and watched.

Cadee pulled out her pocketknife from her flight pack and cut the parachute cords, taking her time to untangle them from the branches where needed. She gathered the parachute, then, sitting on the limb like it was a chair, she stuffed the chute into her pack.

She stepped down the broken moss-covered branches like the spruce was nothing more than a ladder.

Of course.

Almost to the ground, she pushed away from the trunk and landed next to him. "So, I saw that everyone got out of the plane. About where did any of them land?"

He shook his head. "No idea."

"Really? You stood there watching me instead of assessing our situation?"

"I was watching your back in case something bad happened."

Her jaw jutted out. "Like I'm incapable? Untrained? Just a 'guurrl,' like you said the other day when I couldn't lift the huge boulder by myself at the fire? Jade and Skye and I got it out of the way. All of us 'guurrls.'"

He closed one eye, staring at her with the other. Her bright blue eyes were blazing right back at him. That spirit was what he'd always loved about her. Until his anger at her. "Part of being a team is watching your teammate's back. I was *trying* to watch your back."

She huffed.

It did sound awful, the things he'd said, hearing them from her voice. "I didn't mean you are an incapable woman." It wasn't what he thought of her anyway. "I knew I couldn't have lifted it myself, and that's just a way my dad made Mom laugh when she asked him to lift something around the house."

"Fine. I could see that from him."

"Let's do an assessment." He pulled out his phone. "Seventy-one degrees, zero percent humidity." He pointed to the right at the skinny plume of smoke. "Plane crash there."

He ran his hand through his hair. Glanced at Cadee, who was studying the ground.

She slowly met his gaze, her eyes glistening. "If Neil didn't make it...his wife..."

"Neil—he's the best." He swallowed hard.

She nodded. Then she took a deep breath. "Anyway, look," she said. She pointed into the sky. "Heavy bird traffic coming our way. The smoke's moving this direction, thanks to that wind. Fast. The plane crash has started a wildfire."

He scanned the horizon above the soaring spruce trees. It wasn't just smoke from a tiny campfire. It was fanning out through the sky. "You're dead right."

"It's headed toward the village," she said, her voice tight.

"What village?"

"I know it's there." She took off running toward the wildfire.

"Cadee!" he shouted. "We can't fight the fire ourselves. Without tools. Without teammates."

She stopped. Didn't turn around.

"Listen. Like it or not, we are teammates. And right now, all we have is each other. We need to work together."

She turned around. "You're right. I'll be the guide. Which means you need to *keep up.*"

His jaw clenched. "Cadee. I've got a map. I've got a compass. We'll get to the jump base, get the rest of the team together, get to the fire."

Was her face red in anger? Or red from the coolish air of the Alaskan summer?

"We don't have time to gather the team. We have to head to Ingriq Village."

What? He stood his ground. "Why? No. We need to head to base, not wander around."

"Ingriq needs us. Now. It's close to the fire. We need to warn them, get them out of there."

He shook his head. "Let's get back to base, and we can send out a crew to warn them."

"It won't be soon enough! We're going to run out of time!"

"And we have people on our tail trying to kill us! We need to get out of here—now!" His voice lowered. "Come on, Cadee. Work with me."

"I can't. I know this village. I have to warn them. Before it's too late."

Her tone made his heart squeeze in his chest. Her face had paled when she'd seen the smoke rising above the forest.

"I get that. I really do. But what if these guys find us and we bring trouble to the village? We need to get to the authorities right now. Listen, when we get into range, we can call it in."

"No." And her voice even shook a little. "That's my village. Those are my people. Stay here if you want, but I'm going."

He could kick himself. She hadn't just grown up in Alaska, she'd grown up *here*. "You were raised in Ingriq Village?"

She nodded. "We have to get there, Vince. Fast."

"Family there?"

"My sister. Niece." She huffed. "My niece is four. She has asthma."

Ah. A child with asthma and a wildfire. Not good. He could kick himself again. The fire's expected behavior was obvious at the moment.

"Your dad taught us that people always come first."

His mouth tightened. Really? She had to bring up his father? But that was why Vince had become a DEA agent—before he'd wised up and chosen to listen to God's call to wildland firefighting.

Now he was a firefighter for the exact same reason.

"Okay. Fine. I'll try to call Jade and Tucker. You text the rest." Standard Firefighting Order.

She nodded, started punching at her phone.

He pulled out his phone and called Jade. The service only lasted one second, then cut off. Same thing happened the next two times he tried. Then he tried to call Tucker Newman, the base commander, but he didn't answer either. Vince left a message. "No answer, phone call or text."

Cadee punched hard at her phone, scowled at it, gave up, and stuck it in her pocket. "I'll text them as soon as we get to coverage. God, please keep the crew safe."

She really thought that? He scowled. "God isn't going to help us. He doesn't show up."

Her jaw dropped open so far it practically fell to the ground. "Really? You were always such a strong believer. It was part of the reason I never lost hope the past year, because I knew *you* wouldn't. God might not have shown up in the exact way I wanted Him to all the time, but I *always* knew He was there."

He'd left that childish part of his life behind when his father died, thank you. "Whatever."

"Ingriq is that way, Vince. Let's go." She pointed to the east.

"Yeah. What's the fastest way? We need the map."

She narrowed her eyes but stepped beside him, looked at the map. She poked her finger. "Here's where we are." Then another finger poke. "There's the village."

"So, a river between here and there." His finger traced it.

"Yeah. Not far away, I'm guessing. I've been to that river a lot, and I visited the area between here and there." She sighed. "But not often, and it was a long time ago."

He folded the map and put it in his fire pack. Really? So she'd been here a lot. He swallowed, forcing the frustration out of his voice. "Hard to tell on the map exactly what we'll see, but—"

The pop of a gunshot sounded through the meadow.

A bullet skimmed over his left shoulder.

Vince slammed into Cadee as all his old DEA training rushed back. The heat of gunfire. A civilian in danger.

He lay over her, protecting her from bullets.

Had the militia found them?

Lisa Phillips is a USA Today and top ten Publishers Weekly bestselling author of over 80 books that span Harlequin's Love Inspired Suspense line, independently published series romantic suspense, and thriller novels. She's discovered a penchant for high-stakes stories of mayhem and disaster where you can find made-for-each-other love that always ends in happily ever after.

Lisa is a British ex-pat who grew up an hour outside of London and attended Calvary Chapel Bible College, where she met her husband. He's from California, but nobody's perfect. It wasn't until her Bible College graduation that she figured out she was a writer (someone told her). As a worship leader for Calvary Chapel churches in her local area, Lisa has discovered a love for mentoring new ministry members and youth worship musicians.

Find out more at www.authorlisaphillips.com.

DIVE INTO AN EPIC JOURNEY IN BOOK ONE OF

CHASING FIRE: MONTANA

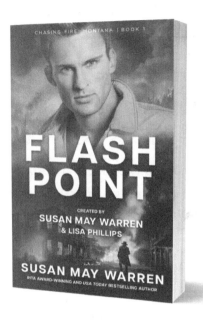

*The Hollywood heartthrob and
the firefighter with a secret...*

What could go wrong?

LAST CHANCE
FIRE AND RESCUE

USA Today Bestselling Author

LISA PHILLIPS

with **LAURA CONAWAY**, **MEGAN BESING** and **MICHELLE SASS ALECKSON**

The men and women of the Last Chance County Fire Department struggle to put a legacy of corruption behind them. They face danger every day on the job as first responders, but the fight to become a family will be their biggest battle yet. When hearts are on the line it's up to each one to trust their skill and lean on their faith to protect the ones they love. Before it all goes down in flames.

We solve the problem of what we read next.   Available on Amazon

WE THINK YOU'LL ALSO LOVE...

 Fire Department liaison Allen Frees may have put his life back together, but getting the truck crew and engine squad to succeed might be his toughest job yet. When a child is nearly kidnapped, Allen steps in to help Pepper Miller keep her niece safe. The one thing he couldn't fix was the love he lost, but he isn't going to let Pepper walk away this time.

Expired Return by Lisa Phillips

 Stunt double Vienna Foxcroft's stunt team are the only ones she trusts. Then in walks Sergeant Crew Gatlin and his tough-as-nails military dog, Havoc. When an attack on a film set sends them fleeing into the streets of Turkey, Vienna must face the demons of her past or be devoured by them. And Crew and Havoc will be tested like never before.

Havoc by Ronie Kendig

 When an attempt is made on Grey Parker's life and dead bodies begin piling up, suddenly bodyguard Christina Sherman is tasked with keeping both a soldier and his dog safe... and with them, the secrets that could stop a terrorist attack.

Driving Force by Lynette Eason and Kate Angelo

sunrise
PUBLISHING

**WHERE EVERY STORY IS A FRIEND,
AND EVERY CHAPTER IS A NEW JOURNEY...**

Subscribe to our newsletter for
a free book, the latest news,
weekly giveaways, exclusive
author interviews, and more!

Made in United States
Cleveland, OH
27 May 2025

17276095R00173